COLD IN THE HEADS

Recent Titles by Gerald Hammond from Severn House

DOWN THE GARDEN PATH
THE DIRTY DOLLAR
FINE TUNE
FLAMESCAPE
GRAIL FOR SALE
THE HITCH
INTO THE BLUE
THE OUTPOST
A RUNNING JUMP
THE SNATCH

COLD IN THE HEADS

Gerald Hammond

This first world edition published in Great Britain 2005 by
SEVERN HOUSE PUBLISHERS LTD of
9–15 High Street, Sutton, Surrey SM1 1DF.
This first world edition published in the USA 2006 by
SEVERN HOUSE PUBLISHERS INC of
595 Madison Avenue, New York, N.Y. 10022.

British Library Cataloguing in Publication Data

Hammond, Gerald, 1926-
   Cold in the heads
   1.   Murder - Investigation - Scotland - Fiction
   2.   Scotland - Fiction
   3.   Detective and mystery stories
   I.   Title
   823.9'14 [F]

ISBN-10 : 0-7278-6316-9

Typeset by Palimpsest Book Production Ltd.,
Polmont, Stirlingshire, Scotland.
Printed and bound in Great Britain by
MPG Books Ltd., Bodmin, Cornwall.

Prologue

I was indulging in one of my greatest pleasures: sitting up in the small hours with a Bacardi and lime for company, watching the grand prix from the other side of the world. As the drivers battled it out in their bid for supremacy I allowed myself a secret thrill of pride. My own small contribution to the efficiency of the petrol engine had aided the evolution of the magnificent machines I watched today.

That was in a summer in the early 1960s, when my powers of invention were at their height. It was the summer when my sleuthing skills were at their height too. For that was when a strange death revealed itself in St Maggie's, our sleepy part of the world. It was, some say, a case that could only have been solved with the help of Lady P, for that is me, though, of course, I would deny that . . .

One

'As grannies go,' said my nephew, 'you must come somewhere low down in Category C, three, minus.'

'Nonsense,' I said absently, fitting the torque wrench on to another nut.

Beau gripped the bolt from the other side. 'You realize, don't you, that Jackie'll have seventeen polychromatic fits if she comes back suddenly and finds him like that?'

'Him? Who?' The job was demanding all my attention.

'Him,' said Beau impatiently, pointing over his shoulder with a ring spanner. 'His lordship. Your first and only grandson. The happy chappy with the crappy nappy.'

'Oh,' I said. 'Him.' I looked round guiltily, but my grandson was sitting up in his pram, chewing happily on the handle of a ball-peen hammer. 'He's teething, bless him,' I said fondly, in explanation. I thought back. I was sure that he had been fed recently, and if he had not had his nappy changed . . . well, he had a remarkably continent bladder for his age. 'He may not appreciate me now,' I went on, 'but just wait until he's old enough to have his own car.'

Beau snorted unbecomingly. I'm sure he doesn't get his habits from my side of the family. 'You think you'll still be around then?' he asked.

'If I can't take it with me, I won't go.'

'That, Aunt, sounds so like you that I won't dispute it, but – here, this one next – at least admit that you'll be—'

3

he looked up at me reflectively, wondering how far he dared go '– less active,' he finished.

'I'll still have the magic touch.'

'Your admittedly magic touch – and mine,' he added fairly, '– seems to have left a certain amount of grease on the poor brat.'

This, I had to admit, was true. Even in the late spring sunshine that blazed low through the big garage doors, my only grandson Toots was greyer than grey. Jackie – my daughter Jacqueline – and her husband had left Hampshire for a fortnight's sailing, and I had rashly assumed responsibility for the child. At the time, I had envisaged a period of peace and of the kind of ladylike pottering which I have always felt I might enjoy if I had time to try it. As always, circumstances had conspired against me. At the very start of his own holiday from life as an architect, which he had planned to spend on a whirl-wind tour of the motor-racing circuits of Britain and northern Europe – and, I suspect, of his female acquaint-ances in the same areas – my nephew Beau had missed his gear-change in a minor race at nearby Downfield. In the din of a packed Formula Two start he had failed, for that fatal second, to hear the car's agony. And so, in a desperate hurry, we were now rebuilding a badly strained engine. Baby care had been relegated to those odd moments when one pair of hands were enough, and we had soon abandoned the impossibly time-consuming rule that hands must be washed before handling the child.

'Don't you worry,' I said. I tightened the last nut and straightened my aching back. Although my preoccupation with all matters of engineering has kept me abreast of the theoretical side, the passage of the years – and, to tell the truth, a certain embonpoint – have made the practical aspect of car maintenance a good deal less enjoyable than I had found it in the dear old days when each of my husbands had depended successively on my help in the pits. I lit a cigarette, patted Toots on his fair curls – leaving them less fair but more orderly – and went out to lean on the doorpost for a minute of well-earned relaxation. From there, I could see the whole sweep of the big estuary, its sparkle patterned by currents and shoals. At the far side, the harbour and village of St Margaret's, usually called St Maggie's, stood out clear and sharp, but tiny. A ketch was beating up from seaward against a foul tide. It looked like *Queen Aholibah*, but John and Jackie must surely be over in the Channel Isles by now . . .

The estuary led to the Solent, and from there to the English Channel. Over the horizon lay Portsmouth, where once Nelson had sailed his flagship to victory in the Mediterranean. Here, we seemed to be in a quiet backwater. But the harbour at St Maggie's was always busy, and there was always something going on of interest.

'Jackie won't be back for ages,' I said now over my shoulder, 'and as soon as I've sent you on your way rejoicing I'll burn those rags, buy Toots a new set of clothes, mend my ways and settle down into a dull and respectable routine.'

Beau looked doubtful and I could hardly object. In the years since my return from the States, I had acquired a reputation for eccentricity. This, I suppose, I deserved. Life is too short and too interesting to be squandered on inefficient ritual. So I neither give nor attend tea-parties, and Jackie's wedding was my first appearance in church since her christening. Perhaps I should have been a man. I've always felt more comfortable in overalls and up to my elbows in grease and oil. Certainly, I find the things of man's world of far more interest than the useless trivialities with which a woman is supposed to encumber her mind, and although I have come to terms with the calculated humiliation of women's clothes, I would rather die than live one of their lives.

Beau smoked with me for a minute, watching the river and the big yacht beating towards St Maggie's, but I could tell that he was getting restless. Inactivity is hell to him – in this, he does take after my side of the family.

'Are you hungry?' I asked. I was becoming conscious of a certain emptiness.

'Yes, but—'

I knew what he meant. 'All right,' I said, 'we'll give the engine a test run, and then I'll feed us all.'

We coupled it to our dynamometer, a weird but effective device of our own fabrication, gave it supplies of water and fuel, and started it up. Inside the garage, the bellow of the unsilenced engine was shattering, but it sounded healthy. We ran up the scale a dozen times in order to get power-curves at several settings of mixture and ignition-advance, Beau manipulating the controls while I plotted the readings. At last, when I had enough data, I nodded to Beau and he switched off.

There should have been a blissful silence.

As my hearing came back, I realized that Toots was howling as if his heart would break. But before I could make a move to comfort him I heard another sound, one that chilled my heart and froze the very marrow of my bones.

It was Jackie's voice.

'Mother!' said Jackie. 'How could you?' There was a tremor in her voice that I had not heard since she grew too old to be spanked. She stormed in, blinking in the fume-laden dimness. 'So help me, I always knew that you were a pair of dimwits, but this time you have surpassed your stupid selves.' Jackie always could express herself, even when in a temper.

'He's only a little grubby,' I said faintly.

'Grubby? *Grubby?* You call that—?' Her voice went up an octave, and she broke off and whirled towards her child.

Then I saw what was upsetting her. The end of the return hose from the engine's cooling-water supply seemed to have jumped out of the sink – even in that moment of stress I found that I was doing a mental calculation of the jet reaction on an inch-and-a-quarter pipe – and had landed in the pram, which was now full to whatever it had in the way of gunnels. Toots had stopped howling now that the offending noise had ceased, and was sitting up and splashing in the warm, oily water.

I uttered a short, silent prayer that the inspection-pit might open and swallow me up, but no such luck.

Jackie, too, seemed to be praying – at least, she called on her maker in a manner that I could only consider disrespectfully peremptory, as she dashed forward to pluck her one-and-only from the watery pram. Tainted water poured from his clothing and dribbled on to and through Jackie's orange sweater and tight, black trousers. I saw her cringe inside her clothes. A clunk from the ball-peen hammer over her left eye did little to help.

With enormous calmness she took the hammer away from him, and even refrained from throwing it. 'I needn't ask if he's wet,' she said. 'In the circumstances, nappies are a superfluous gesture. But dare I hope that the poor little bastard's had something to eat since I left?'

'Certainly,' I said.

I must have tried too hard to hold her eye, for she glared around. The evidence on the workbench was only too damning. 'Biscuits,' she said, and managed to make them sound like camel dung. 'An opened bottle of milk. And an enamel mug! Nothing boiled. Nothing . . . even . . . *clean*! And I left you written instructions, and his meals all sorted out. You'd nothing to do but open the tins and warm them up, but I suppose that was too much trouble.' Abruptly, she spun on her heel and flung out of the garage through the housedoor, nearly braining my grandson on the doorpost. I hoped she was going upstairs for a good cry, but I heard the kitchen door slam as she stormed back. Beau tried to slip out, but I pushed him back. Wrath shared is wrath halved.

Jackie was speaking before she even arrived at the door. 'Hardly touched! So if you've fed him at all it was scraps from your own table. What did you do? Invite him to take pot luck? Or give him a sausage to chew? Or perhaps you left him to forage for himself?'

'It's only the last day or two, while we've been busy, that we rather let things slide,' I said feebly. 'And Toots has never gone hungry—'

'I suppose you expect a vote of thanks for not letting him starve altogether. And don't call him "Toots"! His name is Edward, and I will not have my son brought up under an alias.' She turned on Beau. 'Your bloody Borzois have fed better than the baby – I know who gets the Chicken Supreme around here. You've been eating steak and chips and sharing it with him – I looked in the bin. Mother, this is the very last time I leave him to your tender mercy!'

'Would you care to put that in writing?' I asked.

That gave her pause. Jackie loves her child, but she loves sailing, at least as much and the presence of a brat in tow would relegate her from the admiration which is her prerogative in yacht-club bars, to a place among the patient anchor watching boat-wives. I decided to follow up the diversion with another.

'What brings you back so soon?' I asked.

Jackie blinked, and her mouth fell open. 'Oh. Yes,' she said at last. She sounded indignant, sheepish and defiant all at once. 'We found a dead body. Aboard.'

'What?'

Jackie stamped. 'There's a bloody body in the bloody aftercabin of the bloody boat,' she said through clenched teeth, beating time with the baby's bottom on the boot of my Cortina.

Quite apart from its belated introduction, that statement was enough to catch our attention – and, I hoped, to keep Jackie's off my alleged shortcomings as a baby-minder. Beau stopped pretending to be engrossed with the small lathe – which has stayed broken ever since we bought it in a sale – and I admit without shame that I pricked up my own ears.

I opened my mouth, but Beau got in first. 'You found it on board?' he asked. 'Or do you mean that you found it floating, and took it on board?'

'It was in the aftercabin,' said Jackie. 'Nobody'd been in there for ages. We sailed a whole day without knowing it was there.' She grimaced. 'And then we've had to sail back again.'

As a family we have always had a predilection for murder. Among many other things, we read about it. As far as I am aware, we have never committed it. But we have, on occasions, been known to solve it. And I must confess that the discovery of a corpse in the neighbour-hood, in circumstances that could turn out to be suspicious, and of a sort that might give me access to it and therefore give me a chance to offer my services as a criminologist, made an interesting prospect. At least it would make a change from housekeeping and the little problems in elementary engineering that Beau and his friends set me. Perhaps this indicates some deep psychological failing in me, but I prefer to think that my active brain needs the exercise.

'Male or female?' I asked.

'Female.'

There was a quicker and more discreet way to find out the details than by quiz programme methods. 'Hadn't you better phone the police?' I suggested.

Jackie looked at me as if I were stupid – a habit which she contracted at the age of four, and of which my severest disciplinary methods never broke her. 'That's why I came ashore,' she said patiently. 'I phoned from our cottage then came on up here to see how Snookums was doing.'

I nearly reminded her that his name was Edward, but thought better of it. 'Are you anchored this side?' I asked. 'Or did you go back to St Maggie's?'

'This side, by the old pier.'

And the police would be on the way . . .

'Have you eaten?'

'No, I—'

'Help yourself from the fridge,' I said hastily. 'Poor John must be starving. I'll just pop down and go on board and cook him something.'

'I'll come with you,' said Beau. He had once had a hand in the solution of a murder.

'You can't cook,' said Jackie.

'I can eat,' he said.

'I'm coming with you,' said Jackie quickly. Curiosity seemed to have overlaid her never very dominant maternal instinct, and I guessed that John had kept her firmly away from the *corpus delicti*. 'Just wait a moment while I dispose of this squishy little beast—'

'You can hardly put him back in the pram,' said Beau. 'Besides, you've nobody to leave him with.'

'Well, wait while I change him.'

'Bring him down in the pushchair,' said Beau heartlessly.

'But—'

Beau's eyes met mine. We had but a single thought. The police might be there even now, interfering with the evidence, taking away clues and confusing witnesses.

Seconds later, heedless of Jackie's plaintive cries, Beau and I were in my car – the more extricable of the two – and were sweeping down the hill past Jackie's double cottage, through lanes blazing with late spring's finery and between hedges that tried to snatch at the car but filled it instead with nostalgic scents, through dark tunnels under trees that would all too soon be bare again, down to the water's edge.

Queen Aholibah was lying at anchor about fifty yards offshore. The tide was slack now, at the bottom of the ebb, and the yacht was wind-rode, her chain hanging almost slack in the light breeze. But dark clouds were showing, marching against the direction of the ground level wind, and it was colder.

The ketch looked deserted, but the dinghy was alongside.

We shouted, against the breeze, but there was no sign of John. 'He probably told Jackie to tell the police to sound horns,' said Beau. He walked back to the car and sounded a fanfare. Sure enough, the slightly apelike figure of my son-in-law came on deck, dropped into the dinghy and rowed towards us with easy strokes. For a delicious minute, I thought that we were going to be first on the scene, but as John reached us so did another car.

'Damn!' said Beau. 'It's old Plummer.'

I knew what he meant. We feel that, on occasions, we have been of genuine assistance to Inspector Plummer. He, for his part, has always maintained that we have merely got under his feet, and that when we have been in a position to offer him the solution to a crime it is because our interference has delayed his own arrival at that solution; and his expression and posture, as he stamped from the car to the pier, were calculated to show that he had had neither cause to change his mind nor reason to believe that this occasion was going to be different. He passed us with a formal lift of his hat, a short and inaccurate comment on the weather, and a bland pretence that our presence must be connected with something quite, quite different.

The ancient pier tottered out over mud, and the inspector, who is well into middle age, tottered out along the pier and picked his way gingerly down the ragged and slimy steps to where John waited with the dinghy at the edge of the water. We followed. He stepped precariously into the stern of the dinghy, seated himself heavily on the athwart, and bade John pull for the yacht.

All other apt comment deserting me, I said, 'Er . . . Hoy!'

The inspector looked back over his shoulder. 'Sorry,' he said. John looked up, and incorporated a shrug into his stroke.

'Damnation,' said Beau.

'Instead of standing there swearing,' I said, 'why don't you walk round the point and borrow Willy Parker's dory?'

I watched the dinghy crawl out, bobbing on the ripples. It arrived beside *Queen Aholibah*, and the inspector climbed on board. He disappointed me by not falling in.

Beau came back in ten minutes, pulling the dory with quick, ineffective strokes – he was not at home on the water – and a few minutes later we too climbed gently on to *Queen Aholibah*'s canvassed deck. Immediately, Inspector Plummer's big-nosed bullet-head poked out of the afterhatch. 'How did you get out here?' he demanded.

'Walked on the water,' said Beau.

'He gets it from my side of the family,' I said.

The inspector looked at us with none of the reverence called for by our claim. 'The ability? Or the nerve? No, don't tell me. Just walk back ashore again. I can't have any bystanders just now.'

Beau, on his own, might have given in to the inspector's grim determination and angry glare, but I am made of sterner stuff. I had been carving out a career in engineering when a woman's place was in the home, and preferably in the kitchen. I have bullied two husbands into becoming sportsmen of international stature instead of dilettante playboys. And I have reared the stubbornest child in Christendom. When I have remembered to obtain licences for my television, my car and my driving, Inspector Plummer holds no terrors for me. 'You can hardly tell me to "move along there please",' I said.

His face, never exactly wan, darkened. 'I have been subjected to interference from your family before, Lady P,' he said. 'This time, however, you are not a witness, expert or *de facto*, and I will not allow you to hamper—'

'We feel, Inspector—'

'"We feel"?' he interrupted in his turn. '"*We feel*"? What are "we", and who do we feel? I mean . . .'

'I know what you mean,' I said.

'I mean *who* are "we", and *what* do "we" feel?' he finished manfully.

'My family and I feel that, in the past, we have helped far more than we have hindered you. And I happen to own a share of this boat.'

'I thought it belonged to your son-in-law's boatyard.'

'And I own a share in the boatyard,' I said triumphantly, 'so part of this boat belongs to me.'

Beau saw the line of my argument. 'Which part?' he asked.

'The aftercabin,' I said, stepping down into the cockpit. The inspector was still protruding from the afterhatch like a cuckoo from its clock, so I turned away from him down the forward companionway into the saloon. John, my son-in-law, was smoking his pipe in that infuriatingly peaceful way of his. 'Have you eaten?' I asked him in passing.

'Not hungry,' he said.

'I'll fix something in a minute.' But I turned away from the galley, bypassed the chart table and its covering of instruments, headed through a tiny passage that led aft under the starboard side-deck, and emerged through a neat little door into the aftercabin beside the inspector's large, grey-flannelled behind. He turned round, quickly and defensively, when he heard me behind him, and sat down on the top step. 'Since you're here,' he said, 'you may as well look, but don't touch anything.'

'I'm glad you told me,' I said.

'Sarcasm becomes you,' said my nephew's voice behind me.

The small, neat cabin with its mahogany panelling and bright fabrics was familiar to me because it was usually allotted to me whenever I sailed for more than a short day with Jackie and John. The books on the shelves were mine, and the rubber boots under the steps. But the body was new – that and the demoralizing smell of death, not strong but very definitely present. Beau was pressing into the cabin behind me, so I pushed past the inspector's knees and against the foot of the bunk. In so small a space, we made quite a crowd. With the turn of the tide, the yacht had turned broadside to the wavelets from the rising breeze, and she was rolling uncomfortably. As I swayed with her, the low ceiling brushing my head, a shaft of sunlight from one port flickered to and fro across the corpse.

It was the body of a woman, in a plain dark dress with a worn blue cardigan over it. She wore no jewellery, and her shoes had been cheap. She lay half curled up on the narrow bunk, peering past me at infinity, frozen in an expression of surprise and fear. There were no signs of violence that I could see, yet clearly it had not been a peaceful death. She had been neither young nor old.

'Poor thing,' I said.

'You know her?' The inspector sounded hopeful, almost as if he might expect to find, among my acquaintances, almost everybody in the district likely to come to such an end.

'It's hard to tell,' I said. 'Like that, and out of context. I don't think so, though.'

'I think . . . I think I know her,' said Beau. He turned away, abruptly, and stumbled back towards the saloon. I cast one last, memorizing glance around, and followed him. He sat down opposite John, who looked at him with compassion.

'Upset?'

'A little,' said Beau. 'The movement. The . . . smell. And that appalling stare. I'm hungry, though,' he said, surprised.

I realized that I was hungry too. In fact, by the chronometer on the bulkhead, we seemed to be well through the afternoon, and I had no recollection of having eaten since a light and early breakfast unless I had shared a biscuit or two with my grandson. So, as the inspector came gingerly down the companionway, I moved into the galley and started to wash, preparatory to cooking. Since the galley is separated from the saloon only by an imaginary line, I missed little of what followed.

'Have you had lunch?' I asked the inspector.

'I was just going to when I was called out,' he said, with a great air of martyrdom. 'But never mind me, never mind me. You get used to it, in the Force.' He sat down beside Beau. 'So you knew her?'

Beau lit a cigarette. His hands were steady, but he looked as shaken as I have seen him since we pulled him out of a crumpled car at Prescott. 'I didn't know her. Not even "just good friends". But I think I recognized her. If she's who I think she is, you've got her filed as a missing person.' He took a quick pull at his cigarette.

Inspector Plummer frowned. 'Six months ago, or more,' he said slowly. 'That the one? Council offices?'

'I think so. She was in the County Architect's office,

senior typist, or the boss's secretary or something. Miss Gallagher.'

'Gallagher,' said the inspector with satisfaction. 'I remember now. Molly Gallagher. She went missing about last October or November. We never had what you'd call a good photograph, but the description would fit.'

'She was wearing a wedding ring,' I mentioned.

'She was reported missing as Mrs Gallagher. But the report came from a landlady, not from a husband or family member.'

The inspector lapsed into a brooding silence.

I put bread under the grill, checked on the progress of the kettle, and thought back. The disappearance of Molly Gallagher, I seemed to remember, had caused a mild excitement in the local press and a disproportionate amount of gossip. 'Wasn't there—' I began, but a warning scowl from Beau stopped me dead.

'Wasn't there what?' asked the inspector.

'Nothing,' I said vaguely, and the inspector looked up sharply.

'What were you going to say?' he asked.

John, who had been following his own train of thought, saved me by saying, 'Wasn't there some scandal in the council offices about that time?'

'That's what I was thinking,' I said, relieved.

Inspector Plummer sat forward and tried to lean his elbows on the table. This, being of the swinging variety, swung away from him so that he nearly put his big nose in the sugar bowl, but he hardly noticed. 'That's right,' he said. 'We knew about it. We were never asked to act, but we knew about it. I mean, we knew it was there. There was some considerable hushing up done, on the old-boy network, and I was told to ignore it.' The inspector uttered a noise which was probably meant to be a bitter laugh but sounded more like the groan of a falling tree. 'So we took no official cognizance of it. But we could hardly ignore the implications, now, could we?'

'What implications?' Beau asked. He sounded still on edge.

'Why, that she'd been involved, of course. And that either she'd fled, or that her departure had been made a condition for non prosecution. We're not as blind as people think,' he added complacently.

'She wasn't involved, or only as an innocent bystander,' said Beau reluctantly, stung into speech, I thought, less by regard for the dead woman's name than by the inspector's infuriating self-satisfaction – a characteristic which, I have always believed, is only assumed in order to provoke reluctant witnesses into argument. With Beau, it never failed.

The toast burst into flames. I had not only been too interested in the discussion, I was more used to the pop-up variety. Scraping would have drowned the voices, so I dumped the remains out of the port and started afresh. Even so, I missed the inspector's next question.

'I know how it began,' was Beau's reply, 'because I was used to . . . to provoke it. Later, I knew that there was a lot of "what-the-helling" going on in county council circles, but it was outside my orbit by then, and I kept my nose clean.'

'Until now,' said John.

'What?'

'Your nose. You seem to have dipped it in an oil-bath.'

'Oh.' Beau looked at his hands, sighed, got up and squeezed past the inspector. 'Move over a minute, Aunt, and let me wash.'

'Tell us what you know,' said the inspector, 'while you wash. And hurry it up a bit, if you don't mind. I shan't have any time to spare after the boys arrive.'

'It was after old Lanchester, the previous County Architect, died,' said Beau, scrubbing at his hands. 'His deputy, Alan Bunt, took over, pending a decision on the new appointment. Bunt was an applicant, of course.'

John stirred. 'That's the Alan Bunt that owns *Grey Goose*?' he asked.

'I expect so. He sails, I know.'

'And he never got the job?'

'No. He was good, mark you. He was a good architect, a first-class administrator, and he had the knack of getting the best out of everyone else.' Beau buried his face in a double handful of suds.

'But?'

He surfaced and groped for the towel. 'But his weakness, as well as his strength, was that he didn't have the true Local Authority outlook, beside which the Civil Service mentality looks positively dynamic. Do little, say less, and never make a decision if you can pass the responsibility. Well, that wasn't for him. Quite the reverse. If a decision was needed, he'd give it and ask for committee blessing afterwards.'

'Good thing too,' I said.

'Not for him.' Beau dropped the towel on to the food, and crouched past the inspector to his seat again. 'A dim view was taken.'

'By?'

'Principally by the County Clerk, who's a real diehard of the old school. If it hasn't been rubber-stamped, then it just cannot be. I think he recognized that Bunt was a pretty competent cookie and the obvious man to inherit old Lanchester's job, but he was determined to teach him a lesson about going off half-cocked and anticipating proper authority and so on and so forth.'

'You keep talking about him in the past tense, as if he were dead,' said the inspector.

Beau lit another cigarette. 'In that sense, he might as

well be. He's out on his ear. Devlin, the County Clerk, asked me to call and see him one day, just before it all blew up. He's a devious old cuss, in fact he's nicknamed "Devious", or "Deevie", in municipal circles. Deevie Devlin had got hold of all the correspondence on a matter on which Bunt had circumvented a lot of red tape—'

'What matter?' the inspector asked.

I burned some more toast. Gulls were gathering around the boat, enjoying the bread upon the waters.

Beau thought back. 'It was the new Trades College in Downfield. Shortly before the first students were due, we found that we had to add a lot of extra fire defence and escape equipment to the workshop block. You see, at the design stage the Fire Prevention Officer had powers to decide the precautions to be demanded, but by the time the building was up it had become the responsibility of the local authority to enforce a new set of Building Regulations. As architect for the job – they do most of their own work, but this one was farmed out to me – I had to go to Bunt and tell him that we had to find another x thousand pounds before we could get an occupation certificate, or else he would have to persuade the boys downstairs from him to take a more liberal view of the regulations. The latter course would have been normal for his late boss.

'But not for Alan. Oh no. He decided – rightly – that he mustn't do less than the regulations called for. But – this is where he went wrong – he authorized me to have the work put in hand immediately. What's more, he authorized it in writing, because I wasn't going to have it any other way, and I sent him a copy of the Architect's Instruction as issued, and old Deevie had got hold of a copy of that too. Of course, this had all taken place during the summer holiday when committee processes were almost non-existent, but there were arrangements for emergency action, and even so if he'd just chatted around a bit he could have made sure of some support.

'However, he just stuck his neck out. Of course, he was hoping that the final accounts would show enough savings on the building for him to be able to swallow this extra within the contract sum.

'A month or two later, after the extra work was committed, I had to go and tell him that the final account would be seriously overspent if it included this particular item. So the extra cost of fire protection went on the agenda for the October meeting of the Education Committee.

'Deevie, of course, being what he is, spotted that this referred to a completed building. Either the work had been done or the building was deficient. Which, he asked me, was it?'

'Why did he have to ask you?' I said, getting out mugs and plates while Welsh Rarebit bubbled under the grill. 'If he had all the copy correspondence?'

Beau pulled a face. 'This was before he let on that he had the copies. He just wanted to know which side I was on.'

'You told him?'

He shrugged. 'What could I do? Education work's a big part of my practice. Deevie was established and powerful. Bunt wasn't. Anyway, Deevie only had to go and look at the building . . .'

I put the Welsh Rarebit on the table, with a pot of tea, and sat down beside John.

The inspector ignored the food, as one who is above such things. 'What was the outcome?' he asked.

'Ah,' said Beau. He helped himself to a slice of toast, inspected carefully its topping of molten cheese, and nibbled off a corner. 'Deevie,' he said, 'instructed me to square off the accounts without the extra item, and to let him have the account for the extra fire equipment separately so that he could present it personally to Alan Bunt for settlement. It would, he pointed out with some relish, amount to several years' salary.'

There was a short silence as we considered this singularly dirty trick. The inspector, I noticed, was unobtrusively claiming a share of the food. Tactfully averting my eyes from his shining chin, I looked out of the opposite port and saw Jackie, with the pushchair, down at the water's edge. She was waving, and seemed to be shouting something. My heart went out to her, but I was hungry and I did not want to miss any of the revelations, so I said nothing. The breeze was getting up, and the sky had darkened further.

'Could he do that?' John asked at last.

Beau licked his fingers – fortune awaits the man who invents a truly unrunny butter. 'I think he probably could,' he said. 'After all, Bunt was only a stand-in. I doubt if he had any written authority to act for the council, and even if he had it would only be to carry out such works as the council might determine. I don't think Deevie would actually have done it, but I think he could have.'

'You don't think Alan Bunt ever had to fork out?' I asked.

Beau, without apologies, took the last piece of cheese on toast, and shrugged. 'I just don't know. I had the account sent in as instructed. And then I went to see Alan Bunt. I owed him that much, and anyway I didn't want him for an enemy. I told him that I was quite sure, in my own mind, that Deevie was putting up a bluff just to teach him a lesson, and that if he gave in, offered to foot the bill and promised to be a good boy in future, he'd probably hear no more about it. But he's a strange sort of cuss. He registered no emotion at all, just thanked me for the advice, and got rid of me. I couldn't even tell whether he believed me. Anyway, the matter was withdrawn from the agenda, I know because I was interested enough to get a look at the papers when they went out. And the next I knew something had happened that they were keeping very, very quiet about, Alan Bunt had left the county's employ with a chip on his shoulder and marks on his face, and Molly Gallagher had gone missing.'

'Marks on his face ... wasn't there something in the papers,' I said hesitantly, 'about him being beaten up in the street?'

'Yes,' said Beau. 'About the same time. He made a complaint, but he said that the two men were waiting for him in the dark, and he never saw them properly.'

I looked at the inspector. He gave a confirmatory nod, and passed his mug for a refill of tea.

'Was he really hurt?' I asked. 'Or was it one of those scuffles that men have, with a lot of fuss and no damage?'

'He was hurt all right,' said John. 'He was working in his shed a lot after that, down at the harbour. I suppose he hadn't much else to do. And he tried hard not to let anyone see his face. He was limping badly, too.'

I was going to ask whether Alan Bunt still figured among the unemployment statistics when the forces of nature interrupted me. *Queen Aholibah* was buffeted by a squall that set up a chord of responses in the rigging and made the big yacht stagger.

John got hurriedly to his feet, stooping from habit under the side-deck beams. Danger to his beloved boat is the only thing that can ever cause him to show emotion, and I may say that I love him for it. Looking back over the years, and without the least regret, I can see that I married my first husband for the sake of a J-class yacht. That was Jackie's father, but she inherited only a little of my ability to lavish affection on perfect things rather than on imperfect people.

John pushed past my knees and peered out of the companionway. 'It's breezing up,' he said, and looked at his watch. 'Blast! I've missed the forecast. But I think I'm going to have to move. Where's Jackie?'

'By the dock,' I told him.

'Will you hold the fort while I fetch her?'

'Of course. You might take Willy's dory back to shore.'

'What about Beau?'

My nephew is terrified of sailing, cannot swim, and is a martyr to seasickness. But curiosity conquers all. 'I'll come over with you,' he called up to us.

'Inspector?'

Inspector Plummer followed us into the cockpit. He looked uncertain. 'Just a minute,' he said. 'You can't move the boat.'

'Got to,' said John. 'It's going to blow, and I'm on a lee shore with bad holding ground.'

'But—'

'We'll hardly be interfering with evidence,' I pointed out. 'The crime, if any, was probably committed at St Maggie's, which, I presume, is where we're going.'

John nodded.

'Still in your jurisdiction, or whatever you call it, Inspector.'

The inspector was still unsatisfied. 'If we found a car containing a body, we'd insist on examining it right there, even if the car had been driven since the death occurred.' He sounded as if he were preparing to be stubborn.

'In that case,' said John, 'there would be something significant about the location, and there might be clues on the ground. Here there's only water and a virtual certainty that all the clues are elsewhere, probably where we're going. Furthermore, the whole damn boat may cease to exist as an entity if we don't get the hell out of here, and sharpish.'

'Try to look on it,' I said, 'as a perfect example of the scene of the crime returning to the murderer.'

'If it's a crime at all,' said John depressingly. He had hated his short service as a technician in the police force, and still tries to pretend that crime does not exist. 'There may be some perfectly natural explanation. What about the inspector's men?' He nodded to the shore. Two cars had arrived, and Jackie was holding court among a group of young men, all armed with boxes and gadgets and pretending to admire the baby.

It occurred to me that if Inspector Plummer's minions crossed with us we would all be stranded on the far side without our cars. 'They can hardly use their box brownies and dust us down for fingerprints in the middle of the estuary in a Force Six gale,' I said. 'John can tell them to drive round to St Maggie's. They'll be there as soon as we are, anyway.'

'All right,' said the inspector reluctantly. 'Would you tell them that?'

'Right.' John stepped down into the dinghy and took the dory's painter. He looked up. 'You could go round with the cars if you preferred, Inspector.'

'I'll come with you,' the inspector said. He sounded nervous but determined, like a small lion agreeing to go forth and face a particularly grim-looking bunch of Christian martyrs.

He went back below. I sent a little wish after him, but he failed to oblige me by falling down the companionway and breaking his blasted neck. Apparently I was not going to get the few private minutes in the aftercabin with the dead body that I craved.

By the time that John had dragged the dory up the beach, delivered the messages and rowed back against the new wind with Jackie and Toots, I had the sails ready to hoist again, and the engine chuffing quietly to itself. John had

24

to cling tightly to the yacht's gunnel, to hold the bobbing dinghy against wind and tide. 'Take Boojum from Jackie, please,' he directed.

Jackie followed her infant aboard and grabbed him from me. He appeared to have suffered a cursory wash and to have been dressed in the first things to come to hand, but he seemed contented. 'And don't call him Boojum,' she snapped over her shoulder.

'His name's Toots,' I put in.

Jackie gritted her teeth. 'His name's bloody well Edward,' she said.

With bloody well Edward wedged firmly in the quarter-berth, we got underway. I motored up to the anchor as John worked the winch. The small auxiliary diesel had only enough power to hold her out from the shore so John needed to move quickly to set the mainsail. It crept up the mast, the heavy cloth thundering, and then, as I let her pay off a little, it filled. In a moment she was heeled, bowing to a power greater than her own, and we surged off to windward.

John was busy on the foredeck, stowing chain and preparing warps. Inspector Plummer was leaning over the cockpit coaming, not, as I first thought, being sick, but completing a painstaking examination of the side-decks.

'What are you looking for?' I asked him.

'Signs of the woman being brought on board.'

As he spoke, Jackie came up from the saloon. 'I shouldn't bother,' she said. 'The decks and the cockpit have been scrubbed, rained on and washed with spray, all in the last few days, and if John saw even a matchstick lying on deck he'd have had it over the side immediately.'

'I still have to look,' said the inspector sadly.

'Could you take the wheel,' I asked him, 'while my daughter and I set the rest of the laundry – er, sails to you?'

'I suppose so,' he said. 'You're putting up more?'

'Just one or two little ones,' I said reassuringly. 'Keep her pointed at the big farmhouse on the hill.'

He took the wheel, gingerly. 'I can't do any damage, can I?'

I watched him for a few seconds. 'Not as long as you keep her pointed at the big farmhouse on the hill,' I said. 'You'll have to correct a bit as we set more sail.'

John was bending on the small jib, We set the mizzen and, on Jackie's insistence, took three rolls in the mainsail, Jackie slacking the halliard as I rolled the winding-handle. The jib went up, and I worked my way back to the cockpit – cautiously, for *Queen Aholibah* was well heeled now, roaring along and throwing spray high into the sails – leaving Jackie to help John clear the anchor's mud off the foredeck.

I winched the jib sheet in tight. 'All right,' I said. 'I can take her now.'

'If I'm doing it right, I . . . I'd like to carry on.' I looked at him then, and it was a new Raymond Ingoldsby Plummer that I saw. He had found the most comfortable steering position, leaning against the aftercabin doors, and he was more relaxed than any other beginner I had ever seen. *Queen Aholibah*'s pitching had steadied under the press of greater sail, and the two of them seemed to be achieving some kind of a rapport. And there was a gleam in the inspector's eye which, previously, I had only seen there on the rare occasions when he was besting me in an argument.

'You can bring her up a bit,' I said. 'Lay her on the peak of Briary Hill. This wind and tide are combining to force us upstream . . .' I introduced him to the fine art of nursing a boat upwind, steering by the feel of the boat and the look and sound of the sails, and I watched him for a minute, sharing the magic movement, the silent power of a great boat going well. He would be safe enough until John came back to the cockpit. 'I'll just go down and see how my nephew's getting on,' I said. 'Shall I bring you up an oilskin? That thin mac won't keep this spray out for long.'

'Don't bother.' He was absorbed by the yacht, but not totally. 'Getting on? How do you mean?'

'See if he's sick,' I explained. 'He usually is.'

'Well . . .' He took a hand from the wheel to wipe spray from his face, and ducked as another thin gout whipped up over the weather bow and wetted our heads. 'While you're holding his head, you might just mention that I've put a seal on the aftercabin door.'

'But my oilskin's in there.'

'I'm afraid that you'll have to manage without it.'

'All right,' I said aloud. But, as I ducked down the companionway, I made a silent wish that the inspector might be visited by some moderately ghastly fate, such as having one leg grow longer than the other or his arms shrink until he could no longer reach his trouser buttons. I can be quite vicious when I'm thwarted.

Toots was sleeping peacefully in the quarter-berth – he does not get his inordinate need for sleep from my side of the family. Beau had vanished. I looked in the heads without much expectation, for that cramped compartment is the last to attract anyone suffering from a queasy tum, and Beau usually bolts for the fresh air. As I thought, it was empty and unsullied.

In both hope and fear, I lurched through the sloped and heaving little passageway. Beau was standing in the aftercabin, leaning to windward against the break of the side-deck. Even with the hatch and doors shut, the wind was airing the cabin.

The wind and the sea would cover the sound of our voices. 'How's the tummy now?' I asked.

'Restless,' he said, 'but still under control.'

'Do you, perchance, happen to have such a thing as a fivepenny stamp about your person?'

He looked at me blankly. 'What on earth for?'

'Because, you unobservant young ass who is supposed to be observing clues, that happens to be what our friend up there –' I pointed to the doors visibly sagging under the inspector's weight – 'sealed this door with.'

'Blast! Never mind, I'll tell him a tale.'

'This door always did fly open in a seaway,' I agreed.

'So it did, so it did. And now, what do we see?'

Two

Usually, *Queen Aholibah* enters harbour with the dignified precision of a hearse pulling up at a graveside. This occasion was different. Around St Maggie's harbour they speak of it still, and splutter in their beer.

Inspector Plummer, his thin grey hair plastered to his forehead by the spray that now dripped saltily from the tip of his beaky nose, pleaded with tears in his eyes and voice to be allowed to retain the helm, and John, recognizing the fervour of the new convert and bowing to it, gave his reluctant consent. As we came under the land, so the wind began to gust and to jump around half the compass. Between clawing down the excess canvas and trimming the sails to the vagaries of the wind and helmsman, Jackie and I hovered over the inspector while John got the warps prepared.

But in the harbourmouth a fresh gust caught us, strong and on the wrong quarter. We romped into St Maggie's like a frightened elephant steered by its tail by a drunken mahout, leaving the point of the big boathook embedded in the pierhead and collecting a length of railing chain on the dinghy davits. The fenders being out to port the inspector, who might be a natural helmsman but had yet to learn the first elementary rudiments of seamanship, tried to come alongside to starboard, oblivious of all the yachts' stern-lines stretching to that side of the harbour, and John only seized back control an instant before calamity became inevitable. Even so, as *Queen Aholibah*'s twenty tons tried to spin like a dinghy, her bowsprit passed over the foredeck of an expensive cruiser, and John turned white.

The wind was now strong off the quay, and John had to struggle, with engine and wheel, to bring her up to it without damaging the boat or being blown back on to the line of yachts rolling at their moorings. But the inspector's technical boys were waiting on the wall, together with a police surgeon new to me but identifiable by his bag, and with two of them to catch our lines we contrived to make fast safely. This, however, was by dint of ignoring a stream of irrelevant or contradictory advice and orders issuing from the inspector, who now seemed to consider himself a latterday Captain Bligh and anxious owner of *Queen Aholibah* as well, and I decided that what I would really like would be for him to slip on the teak foredeck and sit down so hard on the samson-post that they would have to use an air hose to get him off it again. Inspector Plummer brings out the worst in me.

The police came aboard and, with a sigh, the inspector relinquished the last vestiges of his illusory command. 'If I were a younger man . . .' he said.

Beau caught my eye. Sometimes our understanding is so close that it is almost telepathic – closer by far than I ever have with Jackie. While the inspector's attention was diverted by questions from the doctor, I leaned against the aftercabin doors. Beau directed the photographer, the technician and the sergeant down into the saloon and through into the after-cabin by its inner door. The inspector would be hard put to it to determine who broke his fivepenny seal . . .

The inspector turned away suddenly from the doctor and rounded on us. 'I shall have to ask you people to go ashore until I'm ready for you.'

John was ready to move ashore, hating criminal investigations as he did. The rest of us were moved to protest, but Beau topped us all – agitated, presumably, at the thought of missing the technical investigation for which he had suffered what he regarded as an ordeal. 'Come now, Inspector,' he said quickly, 'we can stay out of your way in the saloon. You surely can't expect us to moon about on the quayside, in the wind and rain, cold and hungry.'

It was clear that the inspector expected just that, and that his temporary membership of the human race was suspended indefinitely. 'You can go into the pub, and I'll come over for statements when I've finished here. You've never objected to going into the Rose and Compass before.'

Beau looked at his watch. 'Not open.'

The inspector ignored this quibble, as well he might. Jeremy Jaye has never been a stickler about licensing hours. 'I can't have you here, but I'll send you home by car if you'd like. We'll want to make an examination of the whole boat.'

'And how will you know whether any particular find is significant or quite normal?' Jackie demanded.

'I'll ask you later, when I come for your statement.'

Jackie's rage and frustration communicated itself to Toots, who woke up and grizzled as we handed him up the ladder. For my part, I decided that what I would really enjoy more than anything would be for Inspector Plummer to find, too late, that he himself had, patiently and unwittingly, obliterated every clue to a murder. It was too much to pray for, but even prayer can be a comfort.

John stopped off at the harbourmaster's office to tell him what had happened. We others were pressed on by the wind, past John's boatyard, past *Grey Goose* – I remembered that was Alan Bunt's boat – alongside the harbour wall, and thence to the square and the pub. The bar doors were locked, but the side-door was open and we fetched up in Jeremy's small, dark hall, to a smell of furniture polish and beer. Until Jeremy himself came out of the back bar there was silence, and there is no silence so complete as that in a silent pub.

Jeremy greeted us without surprise – we have, it must be admitted, visited him before outside of hours – and showed us into his back room, a real vintage room of leather and mahogany, embossed paper and gloomy lampshades. 'You're always welcome, Lady P,' he said.

'Outside of hours?'

Jeremy waved aside the licensing laws, and bent over Toots. 'My youngest regular,' he said. Toots, being asleep again, ignored him. 'Shall I see if the missis can find some custard for 'im, Mrs Jackie?'

Jackie brightened a little. 'Not just yet, thank you, Jeremy. He's just had enough slurp to keep him going for a while.'

'That's all right then. Now, what'll it be?'

Beau reluctantly produced a tattered and obviously long-forgotten note from a pocket of his ancient and oil-stained corduroys, and we chose our medicines.

With considerable relief, I struggled out of John's spare oilskins – my own were still in the aftercabin with the late Mrs, or possibly Miss, Gallagher. John is taller than I am, but I have begun to exceed him in circumference.

'I hate this pub,' said Beau morosely, still looking seasick. 'It keeps going up and down.'

Jeremy brought our drinks, and tactfully withdrew again.

Over two large gins and tonic and a pint of bitter, we brought Jackie up to date on Beau's startling revelation, but she seemed unimpressed. 'All right,' she said. 'So now I know how the Bunt character came to join the Great Unwanted. But I don't see how Mrs Whatsit could have been involved,' she said, putting down her glass.

'I didn't say she *was* involved,' said Beau, 'but she might have been.'

'But why else would she disappear?' Jackie changed tack.

'Maybe it had nothing to do with it,' Beau said. 'Maybe she just hankered for a change of scene, or the love of her life begged her to fly with him. Or something.'

'Stretching coincidence a bit far?' said Jackie.

'That,' I said, 'is the veriest codswallop. The only surprising thing about coincidences is when they don't happen. I mean, if I could walk along Market Street on a weekday without meeting someone I knew, that would be surprising. But if I did meet someone I knew, that would only be a coincidence.'

'I see what you mean,' said Beau. 'Just.'

'I see . . . I see one possible connection,' said Jackie. 'Could it have been her – she – who gave Mr Devlin the copies of the letters and so forth? I mean, Bunt could have looked on that as disloyalty, and got worked up about it and finally lost his temper.'

We thought about that one.

'Those copies,' I said. 'Were they photocopies, or copy-typed?'

'Photocopies,' Beau said.

'Well, were they the shiny kind like photographs, or the thin brown ones, or the ones on plain paper?'

Beau laughed. 'The thin brown ones. And to save you asking, Alan Bunt's office does have that kind—'

Someone tripped in the hall outside, and there was a thump on the door before it opened. A large form entered, clumsily.

The newcomer was a man in his mid thirties, tall and broad, with shaggy, thinning brown curls and a smooth, keen face marked by scars on each cheek. His hands were rough and stained, and he wore a tattered anorak, short rubber seaboots and indescribable trousers, but he lacked the natural elegance that enabled Beau to carry off an equally disreputable garb. I remembered the face as being one that I had seen around the harbour, but without being able to put a name to it.

Jackie and Beau both knew him. I noticed that Jackie only nodded coldly.

'Alan Bunt,' Beau said to me. 'Alan . . . I don't think you've met my aunt?'

'Lady P,' young Bunt said quickly. 'I've seen you around, of course.'

'I've seen you too,' I said. 'How d'you do? Will you join us?'

'Er . . . thanks. I . . . er . . . oh!' He broke off on the brink of some revelation, and stared at Jeremy Jaye who, hearing a new arrival, had come to the door.

'What'll you have?' I asked.

'Oh. Thanks. A . . . lager.'

'A lager,' I said, 'and the same again. And, Jeremy, I'm out without any money.'

'It can go on the slate,' Jeremy said affably. 'Your credit's always good, Lady P.'

'Thank you, Jeremy,' I said. 'That's the nicest thing anyone's said to me in years.'

'And there's not many around here as I'd say it of.' As he left the room, I thought Jeremy's eyes rested for a moment on Alan Bunt.

There was a pause. Alan Bunt was restless. He had heard something, and I was not surprised. News – and rumour – travel fast around water, and the unexpected return, without 'Q' flag, of a yacht that had been cleared for foreign parts, would be quite enough to set the tongues wagging. I wondered whether to tell him the news. The inspector would want to observe his reactions on being told. On the other hand, so did I . . .

'I saw you heading this way,' he said suddenly, 'and you weren't due back yet, you and John, so I thought I'd just ask if there was anything wrong.'

Jackie was settling her sleeping babe in a deep leather settee. 'We found that we had a body aboard,' she said.

Alan Bunt appeared to boggle for a moment. 'Do you mean that you found a dead, human body unexpectedly on board?' he asked cautiously, with the born administrator's desire for precise definition. 'Or that you had a passenger, who died?'

'The former.'

'Has anyone recognized the body?' I could tell nothing from his face.

'Your Mrs Gallagher.' Jackie's voice had malice in it.

He jumped. It was very slight, but I saw it. Also, his knee was touching the table, and the remains in our glasses shivered a little. But he only said, 'Not *my* Mrs Gallagher, I assure you. And . . . she went away months ago.'

'Well, she's on our boat now, dead,' said Jackie. 'So if she went away she came back. Or was brought,' she added.

'You haven't seen her again then, since she left Downfield?' I asked hastily. 'You did know her landlady had her listed as a missing person?'

He shook his head, and waited while Jeremy deposited the fresh round of drinks and slipped out again. 'I lost my job and after I left, she wrote from Downfield to say that the office wasn't the same any more and that she was leaving. And that was all, I never heard from her again. Poor Molly! She was a good sort. What could have happened?'

'We don't know,' I said.

'She came back, perhaps,' said Beau. 'Did she have any friends around here?'

Alan Bunt looked blank. 'I haven't the faintest idea. I was never on personal terms with her.'

'Would she have come to you, if she'd been in trouble?'

'I don't know,' he said softly. 'I don't know.' And he sat very still, looking into his empty glass.

'I'll set 'em up again,' said Jackie briskly, ringing the bell. 'At least I had the sense to bring some money.'

'Not for me,' Alan Bunt said quickly. 'Thanks all the same. I must go. Lady P, I hope I'll have the pleasure of returning your hospitality next time.' He made it sound like the politest of invitations. 'I saw your article on the effect of tall buildings on the wind at ground level,' he added. I noticed that he did not say that he had learned anything from it, which was just as well for my opinion of him – that article was a catchpenny rehash of a lot of already well-documented facts.

Jeremy stepped back from the door to let Alan Bunt out. 'The bar's open,' he told us.

Jackie, Beau and I carried our glasses through into Jeremy's bar, which looked big and clean and fresh, waiting only for customers to come and spoil it. The lights were lit, for outside the sky was dark. Rain was flicking at the small windows.

Jeremy served Jackie's round, and slipped away again to rattle bottles and trundle casks around in some dark cavern behind the bar.

'Now that you've met Alan, what do you think?' Beau asked me.

'*I* don't like him,' Jackie said with conviction.

'I'm not sure if I do,' I said slowly. 'I expected to, because you made him sound like one of – well – our sort of people if you know what I mean. Somebody who does, instead of dreaming.'

'Of course,' Jackie said, 'you would be predisposed in favour of any young man of diverse interests and an intransigent attitude to bureaucracy.' She said it very well, but with care over the long words. Jackie does not have a hard head, and in this she takes after her father's side of the family.

'Maybe that's so,' I said. 'But we're discussing Mr

Bunt, and not my good self. Well, I thought I'd like him, and I liked the first look at him.'

'But?' said Beau.

'But,' I agreed.

'But what?'

'I don't know,' I said.

'By the pricking of your thumbs, perhaps,' Jackie said. 'You'll notice that Jeremy didn't like him either. I must run along. I'll have to go up to Cecelia and borrow some nappies and things for – er –'

'Edward,' I said helpfully.

'I *knew* that,' she said grittily, and looked vaguely around.

'You left him in the back room,' said Beau.

'Where else?' said Jackie haughtily, and escaped to fetch Tootles. She came back with the poor child slung over her shoulder in a sort of fireman's lift.

'Are you sure you're all right to carry him?' Beau asked. 'You're looking a bit fuzzy around the edges.'

'He'll be all right in the pushchair.' She tried to slam the outer door as she went, and I winced again for my poor little grandson's head.

'She left the pushchair on the boat,' Beau said. 'My round, I think. I wonder if Jeremy would accord me the hospitality of his slate.'

'You could try.'

'I shall.' He whistled for Jeremy.

'Jackie used to have a sense of humour,' I said sadly.

'Motherhood seems to have impaired it,' said Beau.

'She used to have *quite* a sense of humour, didn't she? When she was modelling up in London, did you know that she put in a few weeks at the Leda Club, doing a screamingly funny cabaret act about a stripper whose act kept going wrong, with stuck zippers and things?'

Beau looked at me curiously. 'I knew that,' he said. 'I didn't think you did, though.'

'Not much Lady P don't see,' Jeremy said, coming through to answer Beau's whistle. He had only caught the last few words, thank the Lord. He chalked up Beau's round and accepted a pint for himself. Beau had switched to gin.

I spoke of the weather until Jeremy left us again. St Maggie's is a hotbed of gossip, and straightlaced as well. 'Yes,' I went on when we were alone again, 'I thought I ought to see it, just in case she was going a bit too far. She used to have a tendency to get carried away by whatever she was doing. So I borrowed a wig and dark glasses and snuck in. It really was the funniest thing I've seen in years, and just not quite naughty enough to worry an anxious mum. Not this one, anyway. Heck, the whole county's seen more of her on the beach, let alone those advertisement things. Anyway, as soon as she found out that I knew – I think my escort told her – she dropped it. Probably that made it not fun any more.'

'It didn't shock you, then?' he asked.

'While my first husband was alive, Beau, I forgot what it was like to eat at home. And he liked places with a floor-show. I've seen more strippers and tassel-dancers than you have – and that's probably saying something.'

'But Jackie—'

'Beau,' I said, 'wickedness is in the eye of the beholder. It was a most innocent little act, really. You may remember the end of it. She limped off on one high heel, with her right thumb caught in the catch of her bra, her left hand trapped in the back of a chair, and the other heel still stuck in its seat. And I thought I'd do myself an injury, laughing.'

Beau was actually faintly disapproving. 'Well, if I had a daughter . . . But you will do doubt remind me that, in my bachelor state, I would have no right to be concerned with the morality of any children of mine. Yes?'

'No,' I said. 'But I would say that if you had a daughter

you'd be a damned sight more careless than I think you are.'

He grinned. Suddenly his thin face looked very young, and I felt a rare surge of family affection. Beau gets his looks from my side of the family. 'You're very permissive,' he said, 'for your generation. And a good thing, too.'

'With Jackie married,' I said, 'I can afford to be.' I could have said that I had for years been torn between maternal concern for any high-spirited daughter and an absolute inability – an increasing inability as modern medicine advanced – to see any real sense behind many of our moral concepts, and that, in particular, I had never felt strongly about sex, the act of which had always seemed to me symbolically rather than actually delightful; but I was neither so frank nor so steeped in gin as to say so to my own nephew. 'That's how I manage to tolerate a young buck rabbit like you around the place,' I finished. 'Do you think the slate would stand another?'

'Do you think you should?'

'Do you think I shouldn't?' I countered.

He was spared the need to answer by the arrival of Inspector Plummer, bringing with him a blast of wind that speckled raindrops across the brick floor. He was wearing my oilskins, and looked remarkably at home in them. He closed the door against the wind by leaning back against it.

'I thought I'd find you here,' he said.

'Not a brilliant piece of detection,' I replied. 'You sent us here.'

'True.' He realized then that he was holding the door not against the wind but against another arrival and he stepped aside.

John came in, followed by our harbourmaster Lee, a cheery ex-seaman once mate on a coaster.

''S Jackie around?' John asked.

'Has Jackie a round what?' Beau said.

I said, 'Never answer a question with a question.'

John blinked at us. 'What *are* you two drinking?' he asked.

The question may have been rhetorical or a plea for information, but we chose to interpret it as an invitation and signified our willingness to accept a gin and tonic apiece. John turned for sympathy to Ken Lee, who said, 'Pint of bitter, please, John.'

'That sounds like a very good idea,' said the inspector.

John glared at him. 'When I was in the police,' he said, 'we were only allowed to drink with suspects, while on duty.'

'Firstly,' the inspector said, 'it's about knocking off time if there were the least hope of my knocking off tonight. Secondly, even at the peak of your career you were only a sergeant. And, thirdly, the rules permit one to drink with informers. Take your pick.'

'I think we might qualify ourselves as suspects,' I said hastily, 'for the moment.'

'I thought you might,' John said, sadly. He rapped on the bar for Jeremy.

'For purely social purposes,' I finished. 'Oh, and Jackie will be back shortly – she went on a nappy scrounge. Incidentally, you took a long time to acquaint Mr Lee with the day's events. Do you know more than we do? Because what we know so far would go into about twenty words.'

The inspector nodded sadly. I gathered that facts were still in short supply.

'He told me in about ten,' said Ken Lee. 'The rest of the time—'

'I'll tell it, thank you,' said John. He smiled. When he smiles I can almost see what Jackie sees in him, and she thinks him handsome, although in repose he has only a pleasant ugliness.

'I was going to tell Jackie first,' John said, 'but you may as well know. I've sold *Much Ado.*'

'Have you, by gum!' I said, with a certain relief. *Much Ado* was a flashy and over-engined diesel cruiser which John had bought, with a certain amount of assistance from me, as a speculation. She had been a bargain for her type, but, even so, she was a big investment for a small yard.

'Did you get your price?' Beau asked.

John winked. 'Very fair.'

'Then you can afford to pay for this one.'

'Just about. How much, Jeremy?'

'Fourteen bob.'

John paid, shaking his head sadly. 'Greed is a terrible thing,' he said.

'Who on earth has bought that monster?' I asked.

'Henshel.'

'Henshel? So his boat *Dawn Breeze* will be on the market again? What do you think she'll go for, just in case someone should walk up to me in the street and say that he can't think what to do with all his beastly money?'

John shrugged. 'Two hundred would be enough.'

'*Dawn Breeze*?' said the inspector suddenly. 'I like that name. Sort of . . . evocative. What's she like?'

'Trim little boat. About twenty-six feet, sleeps three, two-stroke engine. Gunter sloop.'

'Can you buy that sort of thing for two hundred pounds?' I could almost hear the rustle and clink as the inspector counted his savings in his head. The birth of hope is usually an easy delivery. 'Is that Mr Henshel of National Fire Defences that owns her? The county councillor? That chap?'

I opened my mouth to mention the long history of dry rot, but John said, 'She was his. She's mine, now. I took her in part exchange. And if you happen to meet Henshel, don't mention the price. He thinks he got five hundred for her, but I'd bumped up *Much Ado*'s price to match, just in case.'

I shut my mouth again, leaving the subject of *merulius lachrymans* unmentioned. Beginners deserve some mercy, but business is business and policemen have no business buying yachts.

John was waxing almost lyrical. 'The hull's teak, and sound as a bell. Sails are cotton, but in good condition. The engine's small, and past its first youth, but very dependable. The interior and decks are rather scruffy, but – can you use your hands?'

The inspector admitted to carpentry in his spare time.

'You'll be all right then. Free advice service if you buy your materials through me.'

The inspector was prepared to rush, but not to be rushed. 'You can show her to me when the rain goes off,' he said firmly. 'Meantime, I came over here for your formal statement. Landlord – you've a back room, I seem to remember.'

'It's empty,' said Jeremy.

The inspector beckoned to John to follow him. 'Did Mr Bunt identify her?' I asked quickly.

He nodded. 'You were right,' he said to Beau.

'Ah!'

'Ask Mrs Hyde to come through when she returns,' the inspector said over his shoulder.

Beau and I had the customers' side of the bar to ourselves again. I glanced out of the window, and shivered. It had been a long, long winter. 'Did you know,' I asked, 'that we are just about as far north as Cape Horn is south?'

'I know now,' he said solemnly.

'I think it's only the Gulf Stream, or something, that keeps this country habitable.'

'Reckon the government's turned it off,' said Jeremy. 'Or sold it to the Yanks.'

'No,' said Beau. 'The Yanks had a meter on it, and we ran out of shillings. That's what it is.'

'I have a feeling that the inspector interrupted just as I was about to say something rather important,' I said.

'Not much wrong with your memory,' Beau said admiringly. 'You were just going to order another round.'

'Ah, I knew it was something brilliant. Jeremy, do us the favour, and have one for yourself. And include our worthy harbourmaster,' I added as Ken Lee came back through the door of the 'Gents'.

'Right-ho. Thank you.' Jeremy's moon-face was calm, as always, but his bright eyes had missed nothing. 'That inspector, he knows who it is, then, the dead person?'

I nodded. Not much news goes by a publican. I guessed that the first hour of opening had brought a steady back-door traffic of wives fetching husbands' supper pints, and bringing gossip with them. 'Mrs Molly Gallagher,' I said.

'Her as worked for Mr Bunt, formerly?'

'You knew her?' I was surprised.

'She come in here once or twice to fetch him, when there was a message. And another time with someone else.' Beau looked up. 'What was he doing in here so far from his office?'

'Well,' Jeremy can be discreet, 'he likes his odd pint, but don't we all?'

'And when she came here for him, did he buy her a drink?' I wanted to know how close they were.

Jeremy rolled his eyes right back until I could see only the whites, as if in the hope of reading the answer off his frontal lobes. 'Gin and lame,' he said, mimicking an affected attempt at an upper-class accent so effectively that for a moment I could almost see the poor woman striving to impress. 'Th'other time she was in 'ere, it was "Monty-ardo" she was after. I give 'er South African sherry, an' she didn't know the diff'rence.' Jeremy's voice was rougher than usual. A discriminating old snob himself, he despises the unsuccessful aspirant to graces.

'The other time?' The gin seemed to have quickened Beau's wits.

'Ah. She was with that professor who bought *Daydream*, when Doc Loyce went abroad.'

'Professor Yarleigh?' I asked.

'That's him.'

'She was never on any of the boats,' said Ken Lee, as if that made it all right. Ken is always quick to deny that any of the yachts are ever used for immoral purposes, although he knows perfectly well that most of the boats in the harbour have had more nylon removed below decks than was ever set on the masts.

I had known Professor Yarleigh for years – a physicist at the university, whose fields of interest had common boundaries with my own – and I was going to pursue this interesting connection when we were interrupted by the imposing entry of a tall, gaunt-looking man in smart, hairy tweeds. He was furling a large golf umbrella. He had angry eyebrows, a querulous mouth and blue, washed-out eyes. I recognized him for James Henshel, managing director of National Fire Defences Ltd, who supplied the gasses I needed for my research, and former owner of *Dawn Breeze*. He nodded superciliously to the landlord and the harbourmaster and, to my surprise, held out his hand to me.

'Lady P, isn't it?' he said. He startled me by using my favourite form of address. I hate my name, but strangers rarely know that. 'Heard you speak to the Association of Gas Contractors. Compression and liquefaction methods. And,' he went on, with deference and condescension nicely blended, 'I learned a lot. Scientific approach.'

I thanked him, using his name – he had not bothered to introduce himself – and apologized for our condition. 'We

rushed away from working on a car,' I explained. And I
wondered why I felt any need to explain.

He smiled, bleakly. 'You were more elegant, last time
I saw you.'

'Do you know my nephew?' I asked.

'We've met,' Beau said.

'Of course. Architect. Met on the Trades College job.
Right?' His voice had a faint trace of the North Country
in it. 'And young Hyde. Another nephew, isn't he?'

'Son-in-law. Tells me you're buying *Much Ado*.' His
speaking style was infectious.

'Yes. Just clinched the deal. Calls for celebration. What'll
you take?' He called for two gins and tonic and a malt
whisky, ignoring poor Ken who took the remains of his
pint away into a corner. 'Wanted to see young Hyde.
Thought he'd be here.'

'He's in the other room making a statement,' said Beau.
He was careful to make sure that every word was present.

'To police? Oh, of course. Heard he'd picked up a body.
Anything known yet? Young Hyde know anything?' He
straightened his long back, as if preparing himself to catch
a heavy item of news.

His patronizing references to John as 'Young Hyde' were
irritating me, so that Beau almost echoed my mood when
he swallowed his drink and excused himself. 'I'll buy you
the other half next time,' he said over his shoulder. Unlike
Alan Bunt, he made the reassurance sound insulting.

Henshel nodded a dismissal, but his face was very cold.

I followed Beau to the door. 'Where are you going?'

He looked bland. 'Visiting.'

That could only have one meaning. Beau has female
acquaintances everywhere. 'Not like that,' I said, 'surely.'

'Why not?' he said. And I should have known better.
Beau will dress to the nines to meet a man, and then go
courting like that . . .

I went back to the bar and picked up my drink. The pause had given me a chance to consider my line of attack. I chose my words carefully. There were certain titbits of information that I wanted from Mr Henshel, concerning both the council and the Trades College contract; and people were beginning to filter into the bar.

'What brings you over here on a weekday?' I began.

'Been thinking over *Much Ado*. Wanted to speak to your son-in-law. Saw his boat heading in, while I was at Freel. So I drove over. Why?' His eyebrows seemed to bristle at me.

'I just wondered,' I said vaguely.

'Umph! You were just going to answer my question. Anything known yet. The body.'

'A woman,' I said. 'I believe she's been identified as a Mrs Gallagher. Molly Gallagher.' I waited, but there was no reaction. You can't win 'em all. 'Perhaps you've met her,' I said hopefully.

'Met her? Where?'

'County Buildings.'

'Gallagher? Bunt's secretary?'

'I believe so.'

'Then I have met her. Used to take me in to see him.'

'I suppose so,' I said. 'You being a councillor.'

'Yes,' he said quickly.

'I expect you're on some of the building committees,' I said chattily.

'Any councillor has access . . .'

'But perhaps you met on business sometimes?' I suggested.

'Occasionally,' he said coldly. 'Occasionally. Do they know when she died?'

'If they do, they haven't told me.'

'You've seen her, though?'

'Yes,' I said. 'I have. And from the boundless warehouse of my utter ignorance I'd say . . . about a fortnight.'

As he was such a tense man it was only when he relaxed that I realized just how tense he had been. 'Well, well!' he said. 'Offer you another?'

'This is mine,' I said.

'No, I insist. Landlord!' He placed the order. I decided that I was forgetting what my mouth usually tasted like.

I waited to get the new one, and took a careful sip. If I pressed too hard, he might snatch it back and try to trade it in on another Glenfiddich. 'As I understand it,' I said, 'she's been missing ever since last autumn. In fact, about since Mr Bunt left the council offices so suddenly.'

'Is that so?' Henshel waited for me to go on.

I wondered if he would accept me as a prattler, even after so much gin. 'That was odd, wasn't it? His leaving so suddenly, I mean. There was supposed to have been some scandal, but I suppose you'd have known, being on the council.'

'I don't listen to gossip.'

'But such a sudden resignation or dismissal or whatever it was . . .'

'It happens. Not always how it looks. Can be a put-up job.'

'What on earth do you mean?' I asked, genuinely startled.

'Someone wants to get out. Bunt, in this case. Wants to go sailing. Resigns, gets his pension contributions back. Fired, gets the council's contributions too. Three times as much. So doesn't resign, makes himself a bloody nuisance until fired. Poor man's golden handshake. Got it?'

I was casting round for a way to drag the Trades College contract into the conversation when our tête-à-tête was terminated by the return of Jackie, this time without Toots. The bar was filling in the rush hour between the end of work and supper-time, when the whole social spectrum is represented, and she had to thread her way round some darts-players and through a blue haze of cigarette smoke to reach us. She still looked peevish. She nodded to me, greeted Henshel and accepted a drink from him.

'Your mother was telling me about your corpse,' he said.

'Not mine,' she said. 'Rumour greatly exaggerated.'

He ignored the quibble. 'Where did you pick it up?'

Jackie flicked me a glance. 'We didn't exactly pick it up. It was in the aftercabin, and we found it there.'

'Good God!'

'I never said they found it at sea,' I said hastily.

'Is the identification confirmed?' Jackie asked.

'If I'm correctly interpreting some faces the inspector made at me about half an hour ago, then yes,' I said.

Henshel obviously felt that the subject had been carried as far as he wanted it. 'You heard?' he asked. 'I've bought *Much Ado.*'

Jackie brightened. Money is a great brightener, and *Much Ado* had been rather a gamble. 'Good for you,' she said heartily. 'You'll get a lot more use of her.'

'I will indeed.' Henshel, in more expansive mood, was less staccato. 'I'll have more space, and more mobility. Small sailing boats are a great thrill, we all know that, but a busy man needs a boat that he can count on getting home in, by a set time.'

It was an old argument, and one certain to set any sailing addict's teeth on edge, but Jackie ignored it. 'We'll have to see if we can sell *Dawn Breeze* for you.'

Henshel grinned a grin that showed both malice and relief. 'Sell her for yourselves. Your husband took her on a trade-in.'

'He did, did he?' Jackie drank gin thoughtfully. 'And just where is my wandering boy at the moment?'

'He was making a statement in the back room,' I said, 'but here he comes now.'

John and the inspector were hard pressed to squeeze through the crowd. I suddenly realized that the evening's session was in full swing, swelled, undoubtedly, by the stimulating and thirst-provoking gossip. The lack of reporters indicated that the late Mrs Gallagher had not received mention in the evening papers, yet most of the yachting fraternity, usually only present at weekends, could be recognized in spite of their unfamiliar respectability. I had the feeling that whenever we looked away we were being watched, perhaps to see if we showed the mark of Cain. And I thought that if one could pick out every relevant fragment of knowledge in that bar at that moment one could almost certainly solve this crime and possibly a dozen others as well.

John reached us a pace ahead of the inspector. He looked from Jackie to Henshel. 'You know, then?'

'I know all right,' said Jackie grimly.

Inspector Plummer greeted Henshel with respect, and seemed to be reminded of his new interest. 'About *Dawn Breeze*,' he said to John. His breath was bated, and I had the impression that for two pins he would have stood a round of drinks.

'I'll take you over her as soon as the rain stops,' John said.

'It's off now,' said Henshel, and when I looked through the nearest little window I could see the buildings and a rainbow, all brilliant against a black, receding sky. When I looked back, Henshel had drifted away, to greet someone else.

'The inspector seems to be interested in *Dawn Breeze*,' I explained to Jackie, in case she had missed the point.

'That's right.' Inspector Plummer smiled, a little sadly. 'I never knew what I was missing, until this afternoon. I've been out in small boats before, of course, but I must admit that I always thought that sail was something mad and special, and that you had to have a queer sort of kink to enjoy it. I never realized that it held such . . .' He paused. Never articulate beyond the needs of his job, he had to sift his vocabulary to express this new magic. 'Charm,' he said at last. 'It's not the right word, but it's as near as I can get. Maybe it's not too late to learn?'

'Certainly not,' we all said – except Jackie.

'The great McMullen was about your age when he started,' I said.

'So was Chichester,' said John.

'Really? Well, if there's a suitable boat going at a reasonable price . . .' Taking the plunge at last, he called for a round of drinks.

'You wanted a statement from me?' Jackie asked him.

'Later will do.'

She tapped her foot. 'This statement I will make here and now. Inspector Plummer, do you hear me?'

'I'm listening.'

'When a member of my family rolls over on their back, it isn't to have his or her tummy tickled. It's because that's what sharks do before they take your leg off.'

He blinked. He has always had difficulty in following the oblique form of conversation that we sometimes adopt. 'She's no good, then?' he asked, with obvious disappointment.

'She's full of dry rot,' Jackie said bluntly.

John and I looked reproachfully at her, but the inspector looked reproachfully at John. 'But you told me –'

'I told you that she had a good teak hull, and that's perfectly true. And she's a lovely sailor. The trouble is that she was only half-decked when she was built, and she's had some decking and bulkheads, and a cabin-top, added. Red pine and mahogany, mostly. There have been outbreaks in the new parts. It's been chemically treated to stop it spreading.'

'But it's still there?'

'Yes. I wouldn't have sold her to you without telling you, but I'd have liked the chance to break it more gently.'

The inspector thought that over. 'But you took her in a trade-in?' he said acutely. 'In spite of the rot?'

John nodded. 'I'd expect to spend three or four hundred, including the men's time, and then sell her for about a thousand. But it ought to be done quickly, and I'm short of shed space and long on work just now, so I'd like to let her go to a competent amateur prepared to listen to good advice and do some work himself. He could invest a lot of his own time and about fifty quid in materials, and in a year or so he'd have a first class boat. You said you can use your hands?'

'I like making things.'

'You have tools?'

'Quite a lot. I never grudge buying the right tool.'

'Then you'd get on all right.'

'I'll have a look at her,' said the inspector, 'and you can take me for a sail. Then I'll decide.' And he paid for the drinks with hardly a murmur.

'You'd better wait and be sure this isn't just a passing enthusiasm,' Jackie said. 'You could learn quicker, and be no worse off, crewing for other people. On the other hand, buying a boat and neglecting it is the most efficient way yet devised for disposing of unwanted money.'

'It isn't a passing enthusiasm,' said the inspector.

'Maybe. But a boat with rot in it demands prompt action. Mr Henshel's been staving it off chemically for long enough. But I know that boat. The time's come when someone has to choose between doing the work and setting fire to it.'

'Don't worry,' the inspector said. 'I appreciate your advice. But if I take her on, I'll do the work, don't you fear.'

'Dutiful little wife, isn't she?' John said with a mock bitter laugh. 'Whose side are you on anyway?'

Jackie said that she was always on the side of whoever had bought the last round.

The inspector put down his empty glass. 'Perhaps I could actually see the boat now?' he suggested.

'Time we were all going,' I said.

Beau, who had just rejoined us, seemed reluctant to move again. 'Surely –' he began.

'Did you feed the dogs?' I asked him.

'We'd better go,' he said. From the door, he looked back. I was still finishing my drink. 'Hey, Queen Rose,' he called softly. 'Home hither, the dances are done.'

Beau can get peevish in his cups, but he should have known better than to misquote Tennyson at me. As I walked past him I said 'Shine out, pointed head poking up through its curls.' And I trod on his foot, accidentally.

The inspector left with John to arrange for a car and to inspect *Dawn Breeze*, and we found ourselves loitering at the corner of the harbour. Although the sun was low the light seemed uncomfortably bright, and the fresh salt air was sharp and heady.

'Are you coming home?' I asked Jackie. 'Or staying aboard?'

'We'd like to stay. We'll have to straighten up again after the police search. And maybe we can still get some cruising, one of these days.'

'And Toots?'

'We will keep Edward with us,' said Jackie, 'if the inspector lets us stay. I don't like that man,' she added.

'If you don't like him,' I said, 'why were you so concerned about him buying *Dawn Breeze*?'

'Not the inspector. Him.' She pointed with her toe. A few yards from us, *Grey Goose* was moored against the quay. Alan Bunt's bottom, showing a strip of off-white through

a split seam, loomed above the engine. 'I'll tell you something,' Jackie said. 'We sold him that engine – it's the one
we had in *Jennie*. And I know exactly what's wrong with
it. But I'll tell him when I feel like it, if then.'

'You are a proper little louse,' Beau said. 'I'm half inclined
to go and sort the thing out for him. I don't know what he's
done to get up your nose so much. Really, the only thing
I've ever had against him is that colossal calm. I admit that
I find that irritating. He never gets flustered, never loses his
temper. It's not natural. If I could hear him utter a naughty
word, just once, I think I could accept him as a member of
the human race.'

'Is . . . that . . . so?' Jackie said slowly, and a wicked
grin spread over her face. She looked just as she had looked,
aged nine, when she told me there was a mouse in my
bed. I was in the bed at the time, with an elaborate breakfast tray on my knees. The mouse proved to be a figment
of Jackie's imagination, but too late to save the china. 'I
think I can fix that for you,' she said.

'No violence or personal injury, mind,' said Beau.

'None.'

Beau thought it over. 'Bet a pound you can't.'

'You're on.' Jackie wandered casually along the wet
cobbles until she was opposite *Grey Goose*. The tide was
high, and the boat's deck was level with her feet. She sat
down on a bollard of ancient stone. 'I wouldn't worship
it,' she said. 'They never respond to worshipping.'

Alan Bunt looked up. He had oil on his face and blood
on his knuckles, but his only expression was of patient
determination. I could understand how he would irritate
my temperamental nephew. 'I am a very long way from
worshipping it,' he said calmly. 'It just plain refuses to
go. The spark's all right.'

'So it doesn't need a new flint?'

'Quite. I was thinking of having the carburettor off again.'

53

'No,' said Jackie.

'No?'

'No. I'm afraid,' she said, 'that you're prey to the common delusion that two-strokes only refuse to go when they have mechanical faults. Not true, of course. I mean, if they have mechanical faults then they may not go, but when they don't go it's just as often because they don't want to go. They have to be coaxed.'

He looked at her, very hard. 'And how would I do that?' he asked. 'Speak nicely to it?' I decided that Jackie was going to win her pound. Sarcasm was a splendid start.

Jackie got to her feet and stepped lightly on to *Grey Goose*'s side-deck. The boat rocked gently. She perched on the cockpit coaming and dangled her feet into the well. 'Oh no,' she said, in tones of utter sincerity. 'That'd be fatal. Remember, I know this engine well. Lived with it for a year, and swung that beastly handle a million times. I know its moods all right. It never did respond to kind treatment at all. What it needs is a good talking to and a swift kick up the crank-case.'

He looked at her again, and I think Jackie was very close to getting her naughty word. But he tickled the carburettor and gave the starting handle a quick pull. Nothing happened.

'You kick it just under the maker's plate,' said Jackie, 'and call it a "black bugger". Then it'll go.'

'Black? But it's *green*.' Alan Bunt sounded a little dazed.

'It was black when we had it. We painted it green just before you bought it.'

'Oh!' He adjusted the choke fractionally, seized the starting handle, and wound and wound until he was gasping for breath. Then he collapsed against the cabin bulkhead, and looked at the engine as if he would have liked to take a very large hammer to it and break it up into little triangles for use as ballast.

'They only take a little understanding,' said Jackie reasonably. 'I do think you're being perverse. After all, what do you have to lose? Or are you too proud to take advice?'

Bunt seethed for one quiet moment, and then gave way to his feelings. He swung his boot in a swift kick at the block. 'You black – er – bugger,' he said. As he stooped to the handle I saw Jackie's toe move, close to the gear-lever. The link-rod, which must have stuck at the gear-lever end, moved with an audible click, but the drumming in Alan Bunt's ears drowned it for him. The starting-cam was now hard against the block where it should be, and the throttle was in its correct position instead of jammed wide open.

The engine kicked, spat, emitted blue smoke, and then settled to an orderly throbbing. Alan Bunt stared down at it in disbelief.

Jackie tottered away. To a casual passer-by she would have seemed to be crying, but I knew better. The extreme of hilarity has the same apparent effect on her. 'That's my girl,' I said to myself, with satisfaction.

Beau groped in his empty pockets, looking for a pound note.

Jackie and John were allowed to stay aboard *Queen Aholibah*, so Beau and I were the only passengers in the police Jaguar which hustled us round the sunlit but still ruffled estuary and paused only to pick up, as a special favour, a return load of baby food and tiny garments.

Beau fed his beloved dogs, the Borzois Cressida and Sol, and we gobbled an equally hasty and probably less nutritious meal. It had been a long, hard day, and I was ready for a rest, but Beau, although he looked exhausted, was caught up again in his feverish anxiety to get the car finished and be away on his holiday. His interest in the demise of the unfortunate Mrs Gallagher seemed to have died of malnutrition.

In a brief resurgence of energy we worked on, but the gin was evaporating. By the time the engine was bolted back into the car it was long after dark, and Beau was obviously ready to drop. I sent him to bed, but lingered awhile on my own, coupling up connections and thinking about Mrs Gallagher. About when she might have died, and whether it was suspicious and, if so, did it have anything – or nothing at all – to do with the council. Could it be an affair of the heart?

Before finally retiring, I made myself a snack and a cup of coffee. I read for a few minutes, a new book on airflow, but was too tired to become absorbed by it – not to mention the fact that I disagreed with almost every word – and threw it aside for a detective yarn. This, too, failed to grip me, and I found that the desire for sleep was fading. I recognized my symptoms of old. Something was preoccupying the background of my mind. The most likely explanation was that I had subconsciously recognized some clue to the mystery, but when I tried to marshal the facts my mind went blank. It had to be something else then . . . And when I thought back to the engine tests we had been running that morning, little bells started to ring.

So I fetched the readings from the morning's tests, and plotted them on graph paper on the kitchen table. The power-curves produced were satisfactory in themselves, but that much had been obvious from the readings. They also suggested certain lines of research for further improvement. I looked at them again, and began to see a geometric relationship on a new basis between power, engine speed, loading, ignition-advance and fuel mixture. I plotted each against the others, and introduced hypothetical variations of valve timing, compression ratio and exhaust length. Suddenly, I had the beginnings of a perfect mathematical relationship susceptible to a comparatively simple mechanical control of the variables. I worked on, scribbling on the back of a sheet of wallpaper, borne on by that inspiration that sometimes comes in the period of recovery from exhaustion. Twice I brewed more coffee.

When I was sure that I had enough on paper to insure me against my usual morning amnesia, I washed up, emptied the ashtrays and rinsed my face at the sink.

At the foot of the stairs I met Beau, slept and shining.

'You're up early,' he said admiringly. 'I don't know how you do it.'

I got him away by lunchtime, and went to bed at last.

Three

The next few days formed one of the rare intervals of peace in a life usually full to the point of hysteria.

John phoned from St Maggie's to say that they now had police permission to resume their interrupted holiday on *Queen Aholibah*. The delay had one advantage for them, in that it permitted friends to join them who had not previously been available; and Jackie had therefore decided to take Toots with her. I could not really find it in my heart to blame her, and said that they took my blessings also. John also mentioned that Inspector Plummer had bought *Dawn Breeze*, and I had the impression that the release of *Queen Aholibah* had figured, however tacitly, in the negotiations.

Later that day, while I was walking Beau's damned – but beautiful – dogs along the waterside, I saw the big ketch running down towards the sea, plunging slowly like some happy hybrid of fish and bird. I would have enjoyed going with them, but I was even happier to have the place to myself. When I turned for home, the male Borzoi brought to me, with an air of great munificence, a tired and soggy looking piece of burnt toast. 'Okay,' I said aloud, gaily. 'So I found it after many days, Sol. And so what?' The dog, whose name, happily enough, was Solomon, just wagged his impossibly thin tail at me.

The true heat of summer was just beginning, in a glory of calm and sunshine, and I took to living much of each day on the terrace between the two big sycamores. I caught up with my reading of the technical periodicals, wrote a couple of articles, lost a few pounds in weight because I was too absorbed to be bothered with cooking, and watched, on television, my nephew getting a rather poor fourth in a minor Belgian race. I also developed further my new theories for racing engines. These were working out beautifully, except that the much broader theoretical power-curves were demanding correspondingly tuned exhaust lengths, and I had a nasty feeling that my beautiful concept was going to be blasted by the need for an exhaust built like a slide trombone – or something equally impractical.

The demise of the unfortunate Mrs Gallagher was relegated to my subconscious.

On the Friday, I drove round to St Maggie's to pay John's men and to deal with any little emergencies. I called in at the Rose and Compass to drink a Bacardi and settle my debts. I was slightly staggered by the amount on Jeremy's slate. I trust him unreservedly, but *surely* I only remembered buying two rounds, or possibly three? I sincerely hoped that at least one of my articles would be paid for promptly, or that my share of the *Much Ado* purchase money would reach me soon. I also felt a tiny surge of pride. When we decide to relax, we do it with enthusiasm.

I found that the inspector had not been letting the grass grow under his feet, at least as far as his new acquisition was concerned. He had ordered a prefabricated garage, and had been promised that a plot would be provided for it; and the men were filling an order for timber and other materials which, at a cursory glance, looked extremely well considered. I guessed that John had been consulted.

The inspector was plodding patiently around, accompanied by his sergeant, making minute inspection of the area and, from time to time, stealing fond glances at the pretty shape of *Dawn Breeze* and her reflection, both moving very slightly on the still water.

It occurred to me that the investigation might have made considerable progress in the last few days, and I decided to have a chat with the inspector. The trouble was that I could think of no valid excuse to open a conversation with him, and I was just deciding that it would be premature to ask him to pay for his moorings after only a couple of days' possession when he suddenly visited me in the yard office and asked me to walk round the harbour with him. I went out, as eagerly as a young girl on her first date.

We walked out to the end of the breakwater in a calm heat that beat back off the water and the hot stones, pricking the exposed skin and making my damp clothes a burden.

'I want to understand the whole layout,' he explained, 'and that harbourmaster just can't understand that there's anything incomprehensible about it. We seem to have established that the woman, alive or dead, came on board your daughter's boat in this harbour, and it's the only starting-point we've got so far. So help me to understand the significance of each part, and why it's where it is.'

'Delighted,' I said. 'Do we know yet how she died?'

He said, rather shortly, that we didn't.

So we walked right out to the light at the end and turned back, and I explained as I went the few features of that rather dull area. Halfway back along the seaward side he paused and looked over the harbour. 'She's lovely, isn't she?' he said.

I thought for a moment that he was commenting on the girl in a bikini who was painting the deck of a Dragon almost opposite us. She was very young and very nearly naked, and I was about to say that if that was his definition of 'very lovely' then she was. But I realized in time that his ardour was directed at *Dawn Breeze*.

'Very,' I said kindly, without even looking. It took the eyes of love even to identify his boat among a dozen of similar size, shape and colour.

He sighed, and I think that he would have liked to remove his hat for one reverent moment, but he made an effort and returned to the job in hand. 'I gather that the Hydes' boat would have lain about here when she wasn't on her moorings, before the trip?'

'Probably,' I said. 'I believe John had her alongside over here several times and for several days, taking stores on board and doing some minor jobs on her. She usually belongs over there – see that vacant mooring? –' he nodded '– but of course it's handier alongside when you're coming and going a lot, even if you are more likely to get bumped by some other clumsy ass. If he was taking on water, or if there was a ship in or due, I'd expect him to go along by the steps. Otherwise he'd be somewhere about here because the ladders are here and because there's an electrical supply handy.'

'But Alan Bunt's *Grey Goose* always goes over there.' He pointed to the far inner corner, by John's yard. 'Surely that'd be much more convenient for him?'

'It would,' I said patiently. 'But this bit is dredged, whereas over there dries out – the tide goes right out and leaves bare mud. That's all right for *Grey Goose*. She takes the ground upright. But a big deep-keel yacht makes a very tricky proposition when the tide goes right down.' It was a problem in many areas of the estuaries around the Solent.

'I see.' He looked around. We were at a point where the harbour wall widens over a small island which was included in its construction. A group of small trolleys stood by a shed, and there was a covered rack on the protective wall. 'Is this part of your son-in-law's yard?' he asked.

'Where we're standing is part of the harbour, but over

61

there,' we walked into the small enclave, 'is space rented by a few of the private boat owners – from the harbour, not from the yard – for storage and laying up. *Grey Goose* is usually laid up here, and your *Dawn Breeze*.'

'Why here and not in the yard?'

'It's a little cheaper, and they have room for a shed, and to park cars and so on. It means towing further from the slip, of course. But the yard's pretty crowded, and John gets their other business anyway, so he doesn't object.'

'It is rather a long way round from the slip,' he said uncertainly.

'Yes. That's why these chaps use old lorry chassis, complete with springs, for their trolleys. It saves the boats from getting bumped. That one's yours, by the way.'

'Did I get one of those? I was wondering what I would do about hauling out.' He patted the rusty old frame with pride, and averted his eyes from the flattening tyres.

We walked on. He led me quickly past the red brick lavatories. He already knew the steps at the corner with the perpetually dribbling tap, and the harbourmaster's office and the crane on the timber wharf across the end of the harbour backed by the small warehouses, but I tried to explain all their relative functions to him. He listened politely and even comprehendingly, although his eyes did stray occasionally to the boats. By the corner of the tall wire mesh fence enclosing John's yard he paused.

'I was going to ask you,' he said.

'Yes?'

'I wondered . . . if you'd come for a sail with me. I'll be working over the weekend, but I could be free on Tuesday. I'll start working on her after that, but I'd love to have one real sail in her first.'

'Yes, of course,' I said. 'I'd love to.'

'I don't know any of the other sailing people well enough

to ask them, and I'm a long way from being ready to go out alone.'

'Just as long as you realize that,' I said.

'Oh, I do. I've enrolled for a course next winter,' he added reassuringly, and I decided that Inspector Plummer might yet be one of us.

I tried to pump him for news of his investigation, but now he found it easy to evade me by slipping into sailing talk. I let him go, after he admitted that the where and when of her death were still undetermined. On Tuesday, however, I'd have him at my mercy.

That Monday morning I drove into Downfield. I parked in the university precinct, and walked to the buildings of the Faculty of Engineering. By virtue of the few lectures a year which I give on the respiration of heat-engines I am a member of the Department of Mechanical Engineering. This is not a particularly remunerative arrangement, although it does qualify me for useful membership of the staff club, but the big departmental workshop keeps an old four cylinder Ferrari engine for my exclusive use. So the professor made no difficulties when I asked, for the umpteenth time, for access to my engine and to the very sophisticated test apparatus in the Engines Laboratory. He only stipulated that I pay half of any technician's time involved.

I spent an hour with the chief technician, outlining the tests I wanted to run and the results that I expected. As usual, he fired up with enthusiasm and promised to adjust his hours in my favour. He also suggested a most ingenious way of cross relating the test results.

The noon class bell had rung, and I had to thread through scurrying knots of students as I walked across the cool quad. On the doorstep of the Department of Physics I bumped, at my third attempt, into Professor Yarleigh, as white-haired and distinguished looking as ever.

'Ah, there you are,' he said. This is his usual form of

greeting. 'I was just going for an early lunch. Would you care to join me?'

This was what I had intended all along, so I allowed myself to be persuaded. We chatted about the weather and the government through two more quadrangles, ancient and modern, and so to the Staff Club. We were the first into the empty bar.

'Let's see,' he said. 'Yours is a gin and tonic, isn't it?'

I shook my head. 'I don't really feel very like gin today,' I said. 'Could I have a dry sherry?'

At a table in a corner, I waited until he had concluded an eloquent and well reasoned tirade against the University Grants Committee and introduced the subject of Mrs Gallagher. 'You've read about our great local mystery?' I asked.

'The lady they found dead on your daughter's boat?' He smiled at me, a little slyly. 'I was going to ask you all about that – I love a murder almost as much as you do. It's the real reason I asked you to lunch.'

I could afford to ignore his last remark. We lunched together, on average, ten times a year.

'I can't tell you any more than was in the papers,' I said. 'Less, in fact, because some of them were inventing details quite flagrantly. It's a real mystery.'

'So it appears. You knew that I knew the lady?'

'I had heard,' I said. 'That's the real reason why I accepted your kind invitation.'

He laughed, with genuine amusement. 'No doubt. In which case, you will no doubt be anxious to pay for the lunches . . . ?'

'You're jumping to conclusions. A most unscientific habit,' I pointed out, 'and fatal to criminal investigations. I heard that you had entertained the lady in the Rose and Compass.'

'How intimate you make it sound! In point of fact, she

was working for me in her spare time right up to her disappearance. I told the police so at the time. And she went over to St Maggie's for me once. I was weekending on *Daydream*, and she was typing up some research material of mine from record sheets in the anechoic rooms. There was something she couldn't make out, so she came over. My appalling handwriting at fault, I'm afraid. She had her own car at that time. The least I could do was to offer her a drink. She was a quiet, very conscientious woman.'

'But you have your own secretary,' I said. 'Why use Mrs Gallagher?'

'My secretary has more than enough departmental work to do. At that time I had a research project winding up in one of the anechoic rooms, with a whole mass of material to be typed. As it happened, I met Mrs Gallagher right on the spot – she was a volunteer for some experiments in wavelength perception in deafness that the ENT Department of the hospital were running, despite which she heard me grumbling about my need for a part-timer.'

'She was deaf? I didn't know that.'

'As the proverbial post. Didn't you know? Those spectacles of hers concealed a hearing-aid. Her sight was normal.'

'I never met her,' I said absently. 'And the picture in the newspaper was very blurred.'

Over lunch, in the long, dark dining-room, we discussed my project, and he was interested enough to offer me some help, together with a brilliant solution to the exhaust problem. We were at the apple pie stage before I harked back to the earlier part of our conversation.

'I didn't know you had anechoic rooms here,' I said. I was interested but ignorant of these rooms without any echo – audiometrics are outside my areas of interest. 'Soundproof too, I suppose?'

'As near as we can get them. And lined entirely with long thin wedges of foam plastic, to reflect no sound at all. Hence the name. Now that we have them – they're comparatively new – we can measure emitted noise without the addition of echoes. So any time you want to do a project on silencers . . .'

'Thanks.'

'Someone was remarking what a perfect venue they would make for a murder.' He cocked an eyebrow at me. 'The victim could scream his or her head off, and not a sound would percolate out to alarm the passers-by.'

'They did, did they? I suppose you wouldn't happen to remember who said that?'

'I think it was one of the technicians.'

My memory, in its usual haphazard way, was throwing up a series of unrelated and probably irrelevant facts. I knew better than to ignore it, for my subconscious usually has a good reason for this performance. 'Don't you have quite a fire hazard in those rooms?' I asked. 'That foamed plastic can be pretty inflammable. I seem to remember one or two bad fires in factories.'

'Yes, they're not without their dangers,' he said thoughtfully. 'Sealed off, soundproof, and lined with inflammable material. However, we've drawn up strict rules for users, and the chief technician in the suite knows that it's more than his job's worth to let them be disobeyed. And then we have a system of automatic carbon dioxide injection, worked by two different types of fire-detector, and another set of alarms to prevent anybody being caught inside when the gas goes in the event of a fire being detected. So I don't think you need have any qualms about accepting my invitation.'

'It wasn't that. But . . . you've never had anybody gassed, I hope?'

'Good heavens, no! Anyway, it's not pure carbon dioxide that we use.'

'Have you ever had any false alarms?'

'Three or four. Expensive, of course, but we prefer to suffer the occasional loss of half a dozen cylinders of gas rather than risk having one or more rooms burned out, and possibly somebody killed.'

'Yes,' I said thoughtfully, 'I bet you do.'

'Would you like to look round them later?'

'Yes, I would, very much.'

'Of course,' he went on, 'they're still rather in the experimental stage. We're making alterations to them regularly, so you'll find them in an upset and incomplete condition. Funnily enough,' he added, 'it was Mrs Gallagher who introduced our architect to us. Alan Bunt, her former boss in the County Council. We wanted somebody who was prepared patiently to follow through a series of minor experimental alterations, and to visit the place regularly enough to keep track of the builder's contract, and he took it on as a spare time activity, with his employers' approval. Are you having coffee?'

'Thank you very much,' I said, 'but, if you'll excuse me, I think I'd like to have my coffee with a biochemist.'

'Oh?' He sounded intrigued. 'Who's my rival?'

'Any biochemist,' I said, laughing, 'or a bacteriologist would do.' I looked round. The room was filling, but the faces which I knew nearly all belonged to engineers. 'Perhaps you could point one out to me?'

He craned his neck to search the room. 'You see the gaunt looking chap at the table in the far corner? On his own? That's Jenkinson. He's supposed to be a brilliant but wasted biochemist. If what one hears is true, he managed to wangle himself a research grant about twenty years ago for work on the effects of alcohol on the virility of the Caucasian male, and he's devoted his life ever since to research with himself as sole guinea-pig.'

'Devotion beyond the call of duty?' I suggested.

Yarleigh smiled, very faintly. 'You might suppose so – a martyr to science, sacrificing his youth and health in the cause of furthering human knowledge. But one gathers that there are certain advantages. In view of his interests, it would seem that almost every penny that he spends is chargeable to expenses, grant aided or tax deductible, or even all three. He'll die a rich man.'

'But tired,' I said. 'Is he Doctor, Mister or Professor?'

'Doctor.'

'Thank you very much,' I said. 'My lunch next time.'

Doctor Jenkinson proved to be an exhausted looking man, thin except for a puffiness around the red-veined eyes. Since he was immaculately dressed and manicured, and smelled faintly of both aftershave lotion and whisky, I decided that Professor Yarleigh's gossip was, if not true, at least founded on reasonable evidence.

He looked up and half rose as I reached his table.

'Join you for a moment?' I asked.

'Of course.' One of the joys of life on the fringe of a university is that once one's face is known – however vaguely – one has immediate access to an expert in any given field, and no enquiry, however unusual, provokes surprise.

'Sorry to bother you with shop over your lunch,' I began in accordance with ritual, 'but you may be just the man to answer a question.'

He nodded. 'Fire away.'

'I want to know whether animal tissue would decay normally in an atmosphere of carbon dioxide, possibly with an additive.'

He looked tiredly across the room for a minute, and then back at me. 'More or less,' he said. 'It might depend a bit on the additives. But most animal decomposition is due to anaerobic bacteria. They wouldn't be affected by atmosphere. What additives did you have in mind?'

'I'm not sure,' I admitted. 'I'm thinking along the lines of the gas they use for fire extinguishing in the anechoic room.'

'Well, they're not using carbon dioxide there. I think they're using BCF, for safety reasons. It puts the fire out, and it's non-toxic. It smothers just the same, but you have a bit longer to live. You follow?' He paused. 'I don't think it would make any difference to decomposition, but I doubt if anyone could tell you for sure. Would the tissue have been kept in the gas? And did it die in it?'

'I don't know. I'm really only speculating. I'm writing a thriller.' It seemed best to head him away from any suspicion that real bodies might exist, even if he was likely to draw his own conclusions later.

'Are you indeed? You must let me read it.' The academic mind is always intrigued by the creation of fiction, perhaps as a reaction to overindulgence in fact. 'In that case you needn't be too much hampered by what I've said.'

'I like to get my facts right,' I said with gentle reproof.

'Of course. Your plot demands a confusion of the time element?'

'It seems desirable.'

'How long deceased is the body when found?'

'A fortnight, at least.'

'In that case you have plenty of scope,' he said. 'I've always longed to point this out to a thriller writer. Did you know that after two or three weeks quite a few poisons would be untraceable?'

'No, I didn't,' I said, startled.

'Not in large overdoses, of course. But in quantities just large enough to cause death, the decomposition processes virtually eliminate them. Speak to Hicks in Forensic Medicine if you like. Sodium azide, fluoride, nicotine . . . Sorry I can't help much with the time element. Now, if you could keep the cadaver chilled for a month or two . . .'

'I'll think about it,' I said. 'And would death from carbon dioxide be detectable after a couple of weeks?'

'Depends. You'd get Tardieu spots, perhaps, on the face, the whites of the eyes, or the surface of the lungs or heart. Not necessarily, and not much. Same with asphyxiation. You might easily be unable to tell.'

I tottered away, my mind buzzing.

Four

N ext morning, I met Inspector Plummer, by appointment, at St Maggie's.

'We've a lovely day for it,' he greeted me gaily as I got out of the car. He was dressed in brand new jeans, anorak, canvas shoes and a hat with a bobble on it. He looked like something in a chandler's window, but at least he had not dressed as for the bridge of the *Britannia*. And he was right – we had a superb day for it, the kind of day which usually only occurs on the one day that one cannot get out and enjoy it.

'You're sure you want to go through with this?' I asked. 'One sail on a day like this, and you'll be hooked for life. You'll never have a ha'penny to call your own, and you'll spend the rest of your days broke, wet, cold, exhausted, frustrated—'

'—and happy?'

'Yes,' I admitted, 'and probably quite happy. Or, more likely, you'll be miserable but you'll think you're happy. The man who described a boat as a hole in the water for pouring money into was right.'

His mood was proof against my prognostications. 'Don't worry about me,' he said. 'I've been a widower for ten years now. I live with a married niece who won't accept more than a pittance for my board. I've no expensive habits.'

'Oh well,' I said, 'you have now.'

71

He laughed. I had heard him laugh before, but not often and never with such complete lack of malice or care. 'Let's go and enjoy the day,' he said. 'My first and last cruise of the season. Tomorrow, the yard foreman hauls her out for me so that they can start work on her.'

'There you go already,' I said. 'You've your own trolley, and if you don't fancy using your car and a tackle you could hire a farm tractor for next to nothing. Dave'll use your trolley anyway, and charge you the full rate.'

'I'll watch how he does it, and then I'll know next time.'

'You won't go far wrong on those lines,' I admitted. 'And now we'd better go before we miss the tide. Hang on while I get my sandwiches.'

We made our way out to *Dawn Breeze* in her own dinghy, in which the inspector took possessive pride. The idea of having not only a boat but a boat's boat seemed to be a great enhancement of the glamour which he had now found in the world of sailing.

'Now, you're going to do all the work,' I said without very much conviction. 'I'm only here in an advisory capacity, or to help out if you get into difficulties.' And I made the dinghy fast to the stern of the boat, instead of to the mooring which would be left behind. We just might have need of that dinghy.

My gloomy premonitions were largely unfounded. To be sure, the awkward Gunter rig was at first a bafflement to the poor man, and he nearly brained me with the long yard by letting the peak halliard slip; and we exchanged paint with both our neighbours before we were clear. After those initial excitements all went well, although I could tell by his desperate grip on the tiller that the inspector was in a state of nervous tension that would have been excessive in the captain of a nuclear battleship while berthing without tugs, and when we glided out through the precise geometrical centre of the wide harbourmouth and met the full force of the faint breeze outside I thought that he was going to yell for the lifeboat, possibly offering me up as a sacrifice to Neptune the while. There is a vast difference between steering somebody else's yacht and skippering your own.

But ten minutes later we were bobbing along without a care in the world, broad reaching down towards the Solent. Inspector Plummer, steering with his fingertips, from the depths of his ignorance was eulogizing this whole new world, while I was inconspicuously adjusting, unravelling and coiling the sheets and halliards. We had little more than bare steerage way, but the ebbing tide was helping us over the ground.

'If we go any further, we'll be out in the Channel,' I said at long last, 'and I don't think you're ready to go offshore just yet.'

'Oh.' He looked around, blinking and uncertain. 'Shall we turn back?'

'If we did, we'd only be punching the tide under power for a couple of hours, and we'd get back to the harbour while the water was too low to get inside. I suggest we anchor up for a couple of hours and have lunch in peace.'

'We'll do that,' he said, relieved and decisive.

I showed him how to flake the chain and to stock and drop the anchor clear, and we swung gently at anchor just outside Freel harbour. Freel has water at all states of the tide, and we were rocked pleasantly by the occasional fishing boat headed in for market, pursued by its train of screaming seabirds. A coaster thumped by upriver, and a tanker passed far out at sea. We could hear the noises ashore, just loud enough to make us glad to be away from them.

We ate our sandwiches. The inspector, astonishingly, had brought a bottle of wine, and, burgeoning under the combined influences of wine, sunshine and a kind of spontaneous enthusiasm that for long had been missing from his life, he became gay and almost flirtatious. The brewing of coffee he left to me, and rowed his dinghy to the rocks for limpet bait. He arrived back puffing, after a hard pull against the tide, and settled down on deck to fish inexpertly.

I gave him his coffee. There was too much silence. If there had been any conversation, I could have dragged the late Mrs Gallagher into it somehow, but he was fishing and oblivious. But eventually I jumped in with both feet, as they say. 'Has the investigation made any progress?' I asked.

To my surprise he showed no irritation at this intrusion of work and worry into the calm of his special day. It was as if the relaxation induced by this environment was enough to obliterate even the frustration of that frustrating case.

'Very little,' he said calmly. 'We've traced her through her earlier years, without learning anything significant. There was a man in her life many years ago, but no wedding ring – she seems to have adopted the "Mrs" as an honorary title. The man married her best friend, and they live happily near Belfast and haven't been in England since the Coronation.

'We've found no trace of the lady at all between her disappearance and when your daughter went down into the aftercabin for a pad of weather report cards, and found her. And no witnesses have been found who saw her go, or be taken, on board.'

He put down his empty mug, and resumed fishing.

I lit a cigarette, and watched the smoke in the light breeze. 'When was she last seen precisely?' I asked.

'October eighth. She left her work as usual, had a meal on her own at a café, and then drove away in her car. The car was later found near the public garage where she kept it, but nobody had seen it being parked.'

'Of course,' I said casually, 'you checked on whether she'd been over to Professor Yarleigh's anechoic rooms at the university?'

'We did, and she hadn't.'

I decided that, come hell or high water, I was going to surprise the inspector before this conversation ended. 'Anything odd on her last day at work?' I asked.

'Nothing that we can be sure is significant. Some phone calls, from sources unknown. Several visitors, all identified except one, a man who knew his way in and went straight to see her. We're still trying to get more about him, but after all this time . . .'

'And at this end of the time-scale?'

'Nothing. Absolutely nothing. We've spoken to everyone we know of who could have been around the harbour. Nothing.'

'Did anybody mention Geoff Allen to you?' I asked, on a sudden thought.

'No. Why? Should they have?'

'Back in October, he was living aboard his boat. He used to be the bank manager in Downfield. Retired now.'

He frowned in puzzlement. 'Why do you mention him specifically?'

I shrugged. 'I don't know. He might have seen something.'

'It's the period of two to four weeks ago that we want witnesses for. There's no indication at all that—' He broke off as the line in his hand began to jerk and vibrate, and I left him in peace. The first time that a man catches a fish from the deck of his own boat constitutes a sacred moment.

He hauled up a monster of some seven inches, and looked at it with mingled pride and awe as it jiggled on the hook. 'What is it?' he asked. 'A codling?'

'A coalfish,' I told him.

'Oh. Can one eat it?'

'One can. If one enjoys eating fried cotton wool. Or boiled, of course, according to taste.'

He detached it gingerly, and threw it back.

'Your best hope probably lies in the medical report,' I prompted him.

He grunted, but quite amiably. 'It's a pretty thin hope. She'd been dead not more than a month, perhaps as little as a fortnight, depending on the prevailing temperature. That's the best they'll give me. And decomposition was advanced far enough to prevent the pathologist being certain as to the cause of death. He thinks she may have been asphyxiated.'

'Tardieu spots?' I asked knowledgeably.

He was still unsurprised. 'Yes,' he said, 'he thinks so. One or two, on a lung. The rest of the report was taken up with old operations and minor physical defects except for one rather interesting thing. He thinks that she was moved after death. The post-mortem lividity doesn't quite match the position that she was found in. Nearly, but not quite. It would be fixed, of course, after about twelve hours. He suggested that she had been lying in a more curled up position than that in which we found her.'

'But he wasn't sure?'

'No.'

He fished quietly. I threw my cigarette end irritably at an impertinent looking gull and lit another. 'You'll have to consider carbon dioxide poisoning,' I said.

'It has been mentioned. But how?'

'You knew, of course, that the anechoic rooms – where she used to do volunteer work in the evening – have automatic gas injection for firefighting? And that they've had some false alarms? She was deaf – perhaps she didn't hear the alarm and got caught?'

'I didn't. Interesting, of course, but rather remote in time and space. Over six months ago. I shall think, and enquire,' he finished, with maddening calmness.

'Do that,' I said. 'And while you're thinking, think also on the fact that some poisons are virtually destroyed early in the decomposition processes.'

'He said that he could find no traces of any poison.'

'That isn't quite the same thing. Ask him if he could have spotted a barely lethal dose of say nicotine or – er – sodium azide.'

'I will.' And the inspector shut his mouth firmly, and concentrated on the absent fish.

'Any more facts?' I asked. 'Or theories?'

'No facts at all, and you must know that I couldn't possibly discuss theories with you. But to be quite frank if we get no more evidence we may have to settle for an unsolved death with a "police have not ruled out foul play" implication and an open verdict.'

'Verdict? That reminds me, when is the inquest?'

'Thursday. Your daughter and her husband are flying back to testify, and that's about all the evidence there will be. So it'll be hardly worth your while coming.'

'I'll probably come anyway.'

'Probably,' he agreed. The line jumped in his fingers, and he hauled up another fish. 'Coalfish,' he said disgustedly, and threw it back.

I tried, one last time, to keep the discussion alive. 'To me,' I said, 'it seems very significant that she vanished so many months ago and reappeared, several weeks dead, in a place where she could not have lain for very long, was probably moved after death, and there is no sign at all of her having been alive during the interim. Had you considered that she might have been kept on ice all winter?'

He sighed. 'Strange as it may seem to you,' he said, 'that possibility has not been overlooked, far-fetched though it is. But the nearest freezing plant is about five miles away, and they turned over the contents of each of its rooms a dozen times during the winter. And now—'

'You've had enough?' I suggested. When Inspector Plummer becomes sarcastic, he's had enough.

'Frankly, yes. In gratitude for your help I've indulged your curiosity –' I wondered at that point whether now to reveal to him that his last fish had been a codling '– but now I'd like to continue enjoying my day off, in my own boat, on a lovely day, and in the company of a charming lady.'

I gave him the benefit of any doubt that his last remark was sarcastically intended. 'Thank you,' I said.

Still jiggling the line with his right hand, he leaned back against the cabin top and studied his left hand. 'I've been meaning to ask you what this white stuff is,' he said, brushing a white powdering off his leg.

'That's the prophylactic against dry rot,' I told him. 'That kind of damage is often triggered off by rain or dew finding its way through the deck. Rot needs fresh water dampness to get it started. When a boat's laid up in the winter, rain may get through its covers, and you can get a lot of condensation. So a sprinkling of fungicide on deck makes sure that any water finding its way below carries the stuff along with it.'

'But this isn't the winter.'

'No. But *Dawn Breeze* was launched very late this year. And you'll notice that the only traces are where the cockpit cover would have sheltered the deck from rain, just beside the coaming. So you still have last year's sodium fluoride—' I broke off.

'Is that what it is? The stuff they put in water supplies for the sake of our teeth?'

'Yes. A lot of them use it around the harbour. And it's also one of the poisons which are unlikely to be traced after the body has begun to decay. And now,' I said, 'just relax and enjoy your day off in your own boat, on a lovely day, and so on and so forth.'

I drove home in the cool of the evening. I was happily tired, but feeling the effect of a long day in a small boat and under a hot sun.

A small and elderly Ford was parked outside the front door, and a small and elderly figure was perched on my canvas chaise longue under the sycamore but jumped up and came to meet me as I left the car. Although it had been several years since we had last met, Mr MacKillop – Mac to his friends – had not changed. I had first met him when he acted as clerk of works on several of my nephew's projects. He then settled at Downfield Hospital as permanent master of works, lording it, in his humble Scots way, over staff, direct labour and contractors alike. Despite an almost complete lack of common interests, Mac and I had developed a mutual respect and liking.

'Good evening, Mac,' I said happily. 'Lovely to see you again! I hope you haven't been waiting long?'

'Not very long,' he said, crinkling his kindly face in the smile which he never bestows lightly. 'An hour, maybe. And very pleasantly spent, in this weather and in this beautiful spot.'

I looked at the garden, with a certain amount of shame. 'Beautiful it may be,' I said, 'but it's getting out of hand again. It's time I hired a couple of men with machetes or whatever it is one slashes one's way through the jungle with. It's just that we've been rather busy this year and it got away from us.'

Mac chuckled. 'And just when was the last time you wasna' over busy to work in the garden?' he asked.

'Donkey's years,' I admitted after a moment's thought. 'But, Mac, if you've been waiting an hour, which probably means longer, you must have come straight from your work.'

'Aye.'

'You must be starving, then. Stay and have a bite with

me, and then you can tell me what brings you over this way.'

'Och, I'd not like to bother your ladyship,' he said, with a humility that left me, as always, feeling ashamed. I do not demand more than common courtesy from anyone.

'Nonsense, Mac,' I said brusquely. 'I was just going to make something for myself, and it's no more trouble to cook for two than for one. And if you won't join me, I'll have to go hungry until you've told me all about it. Anyway, I'd be glad of the company.'

He gave in, with natural grace. I think that I'm the only person from whom Mac will accept a little gentle bullying. We shared a couple of codling – the inspector had started to fish with success just before we started back – and a large bottle of Beau's beer, then we went back into the garden to watch the soft, rich light changing as the sun crawled down the sky, and we chatted about old friends, until gradually Mac fell silent and I knew he was ready to speak of what was on his mind.

Mac knocked out his pipe and cleared his throat. 'I came,' he said slowly, 'about the lassie that Miss Jackie found in the boat.'

'Mrs Gallagher? You didn't know her did you, Mac? Not one of your old flames?'

'Och no. But I'm called to be on the jury at the inquest, and I thought I should maybe know a wee bit more of the background. There can't be any objection to my learning all that I can, before the enquiry starts.'

'I suppose not,' I said doubtfully. 'What do you want to know?'

'What can you tell me?'

'You're really only supposed to go on the evidence presented . . .'

'But the jury can ask questions?'

'I suppose so,' I said.

'Well, I can't ask the right questions if I don't know what's not been said,' Mac said reasonably.

I had a feeling that the law did not encourage a prospective juror to do his own researches, but Mac was determined and I was compliant. I gave him all the real facts as I knew them – and as he would almost certainly hear them at the inquest – and listened while he considered aloud their implications. The long gap between the dead woman's last known public appearance and the apparent time of her death seemed as significant to him as it had to me.

'You think she was in cold storage, do you no?' Mac asked.

'I never said that,' I said hastily.

'No. You didn't say it. But if yon inspector told you that she hadn't been in Lane's plant, it's because you asked him; and if you asked him it's because you thought she might have been. And a very reasonable suggestion it is.'

I hesitated. 'Well,' I said, 'at least it's a simple and easy way to explain such a total disappearance over a period of about eight months. Inspector Plummer thinks otherwise.'

'Aye, he would.' Mac's tone was dry. The two men had clashed before. 'And he may have checked Lane's place, but does he not know how many cold rooms there are at the university, and in the shops? Dozens. And she was working up at the university in her evenings. And there's many a big house with its own big freezer. And, I wonder, did he look into the National Fire Defences gas plant? All that dry ice?'

'Councillor Henshel's place,' I said thoughtfully. 'Does he have much gas plant? I thought he was concerned with foam extinguishers and alarm systems and hose reels.'

'You should see it,' Mac said shortly. 'Lady P, yon man has the agency for bulk handling of all the bottled gasses and dry ice for the area. He supplies the medical gasses to the hospital too.'

'I'll tell you something else,' I said. 'He was in the pub just after we brought the body in. He seemed to know something, and to be very interested.'

'Did he, now?' Mac sounded troubled. 'Yon's not a good man, Lady P,' he said earnestly. 'He's ruthless. He has a bit of power, he knows it, and he uses it.'

'He struck me that way too, a bit,' I said, although the worst that I knew of him was that he was the type of petty fixer that thrives in local politics, always ready to trade one favour for another, particularly in liquor licences and professional appointments but occasionally rising to traffic in planning consents and public contracts.

'More than a bit,' Mac said. 'I know him, Lady P. His firm delivers the gasses to the hospital, and it's my job to accept them. The cylinders weren't always full, because the valves leak a wee bit. The older the cylinder the less gas it'll have in it. I objected, but his firm told me that once I'd taken the cylinders I was to be charged the full price. So I got a gauge, and I tested them on the lorry, and I only took the fullest,' he said complacently.

'What happened?' I asked, greatly intrigued.

Mac chuckled. 'The men didn't' like it, but I wouldn't take the gasses otherwise. At the next visit, a young manager chappie came with them, and I told him I'd pick my own cylinders or he could take the something lot back an' I'd complain to the Board that I couldna' get a good service. And I did it my own way again. Then, two days after, along comes His Nibs to see the Administrator. He'd been to the Super, an' got no change there.

'I was called in. In my presence, he told the Administrator that valves always leak a bit under pressure – which is true enough – and that his men filled the bottles full, but he couldn't guarantee that they was still full when they got to the customer. He said that the bit that was missing was very small. So I said that we quite understood that, and we'd accept the ones as was nearest full. Then Henshel asked the Administrator, very reasonably, what'd happen if all his customers said that, and I said as he'd have to get better valves and no be letting our expensive gasses leak away, or he could fill the cylinders oftener, or that we'd accept a discount for lost weight.

'Henshel got a bit angry then, and said that we'd have to take what we got and like it, and I said as I'd recommend to the Board that quotations be taken again on the basis of full cylinders and an appraisal made. The Administrator was trying not to grin all o'er his face, for he canna' stand Henshel.

'Then Henshel shook the Administrator's hand, but he didna' shake mine, and he left.

'The very next day, Henshel got hold of a member of the Board, some kind of a business acquaintance, and walked him round the hospital in his capacity as councillor, drawing attention to any little defect he could find. There wasn't much, but he made the most of what there was.

'I got word of what was up, and I hurried to meet them at the corner of the service yard. The Board member was looking very tired. And, right there, Henshel points to a bit of wall that was down, and said as it had been down for weeks.

'"It hasna' that," I says. "It was your own driver as knocked that down yesterday, and the builder comes the morn. I'll be sending you his account." And young Keele, my assistant, bore me out. He better,' Mac added grimly.

'And was it really the driver that knocked the wall down?' I asked.

'As to that,' Mac said blandly, 'I'm no sayin', although the whole business was a bit of luck for the laddie as drives the tanker. We've had full cylinders ever since, and

I showed Mr Henshel that I could play rough games and all, but I've had to move out of the house the council gave me. The rent was up and the rates were up, and no maintenance done. I'm over the council's boundary now, and all's well. But yon's an arrogant man, Lady P, a ruthless man.'

After Mac had gone I thought long and hard about Henshel. I supposed he supplied the fire-fighting gas for the anechoic rooms, but apart from that fact, and that he was ruthless when it came to getting his own way, there was nothing at all to connect him with Mrs Gallagher.

The inquest was held in a rundown hall in Downfield, before a coroner who turned out to be a quick-witted lawyer whom I had met once before at some reception. A number of reporters were in the hall, and as many of the public as could find a place. I reached the hall in good time, and settled myself into a seat and looked around. I saw many faces that I recognized. Alan Bunt, large and sweaty and ill-dressed, looking down at his meaty hands. Geoff Allen looking relaxed and tanned in an open-necked shirt. Henshel, too, shaking hands with people, making sure that he chatted up all who might he useful to him. There were other faces too, from the university, who might have known Mrs Gallagher.

John and Jackie had flown back the night before, looking fit and brown, leaving Toots in the care of their shipmates. Jackie was the first witness, testifying to the finding of the body. She spoke her piece well and convincingly, so that she was dismissed after a couple of minor questions concerning the boat's movements. She was followed by a succession of police witnesses, including Inspector Plummer, testifying as to receiving the call, arriving at the boat, and examining and recording the body. In answer to a question, the inspector admitted that his investigations had produced no trace of the lady's movements for many months prior to the finding of her body.

The main witness of the day was the pathologist, a bald, untidy man whom I remembered seeing around the university on occasions. He was barely halfway through his brief testimony on the condition of the body before I saw Mac whispering urgently in the foreman's ear. The foreman frowned, asked a question, and then nodded, and Mac winked broadly at me. Several heads turned in my direction, including Inspector Plummer's. When the pathologist finished his evidence by stating that he was unable to determine the cause of death, the foreman rose to his feet and addressed the coroner.

'The jury would like to ask the witness, Sir, whether – er – he made any tests to see whether the deceased had been preserved by refrigeration.'

The coroner absorbed the idea without showing any surprise. 'In view of the time elapsed between the disappearance of the deceased and the apparent time of death, the question would seem to be a reasonable one, but I will rephrase it. Dr Rodnan, if the victim had died last autumn, and had been preserved against putrefaction by a lowering of the temperature, would you have expected to detect the fact, or could you still do so?'

The police solicitor, who also acts for me on occasions, started to rise and then checked himself. The reporters busied themselves over their notes.

The witness hesitated. 'I . . . I can't give an explicit answer,' he said. 'There were no signs of freezing.'

'Would you expect to see . . . "signs"?'

'That would depend on the degree of freezing. Prolonged deep-freezing I think I would have detected, although remarkable individual variations can occur. But if the body had merely been chilled . . .'

'Yes, what then?' the coroner asked.

'Some superficial dehydration, perhaps, and other very small signs. But with decomposition already advanced as far as it had before I saw the body, no I don't think I would expect to detect the fact, and although I will make a further examination with this suggestion in mind I would not expect it to confirm or deny the supposition.'

'You mean that you cannot tell whether or not the body has been dead for a matter of some eight months or so, instead of the apparent three weeks?'

'That's so.'

The hall was filled with the rustle of many whispers, and someone laughed softly.

An hour later, predictably, the inquest was adjourned for further police enquiries.

With equal predictability, Inspector Plummer caught up with me in the hallway before I could escape to the car park. 'You put that damned old heathen up to asking whether she could have been kept in a freezer,' he growled.

I tried to move back out of the thick of the crowd. 'I didn't,' I said. 'But if I had, would it have mattered?'

'You should know by now that I don't like having my investigations hampered by reporters and publicity, especially speculation about a ridiculous theory like that.'

'It isn't a theory,' I said patiently, 'I didn't propound it, and if you're so sure that it's ridiculous then you should appreciate that the publicity should do more good than harm. For instance, it might bring forward somebody who'd seen her during the winter.'

He glowered. 'And they mightn't come forward at all. If the papers start hinting that she's been dead since autumn, somebody who thought they'd seen her during the winter might decide that they must have been mistaken. No, publicity was the last thing—'

'If you don't want publicity,' I interrupted gently, 'hadn't you better pipe down?'

He glanced round at a ring of interested faces, cast up his eyes, muttered something about meddling women, and stamped away.

It seemed that my short romance was ended.

Five

I returned home.

John and Jackie had fled to catch a plane back to
Queen Aholibah and Toots, and the brief contact with
them had underlined the solitude of my present existence.
Usually I thrive on solitude, but for reasons which I could
only guess at later I now found it disturbing. When I had
eaten and done the few remaining chores I was too restless and too conscious of the house's emptiness to settle
with a book or in front of the television. I paced the
house for a while with my stomach full of nerves, and
wondered whether Inspector Plummer was sitting at ease
in his niece's house sticking pins in a little wax effigy
of me. I was very conscious of the sticky warmth of the
evening.

As always when disturbed, I found solace in the workshop part of the garage, although the emptiness of that
large space with Beau away reminded me again that I was
alone. There, using my hands and my brain on my chosen
interests, I can lose myself, far from stresses born of
mankind. I put on an overall and started pottering.

My designs for the new parts were still only in the form
of rough sketches, but the geometry and dimensions were
established. I drafted my sketches straight on to sheet
metal and started fabricating. The hardest part of any
project, yet the most fascinating part, is the big jump from
the drawing-board towards reality. Whether you know the

road or not, you must start the journey if you are ever to complete it.

Time dribbled away – as it does, especially through my heedless fingers when I am fully occupied.

Some time later I was listening to light music on the radio, brazing some parts, and at the same time thinking out the next stages of development. Although it was long after dark, the big garage doors were slid fully open for acoustic reasons and in an attempt to find a little air on that hot, airless night.

When the electricity was turned off – from the fuse-box in the hall, we learned later – it was the dying of the big radio on its shelf that first made me aware of the change, for the seam that I was brazing was incandescent while the dark blue goggles made darkness of everything outside the flame. I finished the seam, and turned, keeping the small flame burning for the sake of what little light it shed.

As I turned, I heard a stealthy footstep in the garage.

I spun round the rest of the way, pushing the blue goggles up on to my forehead. It was pitch dark, the open end of the garage darker even than the interior where the faint light from the hissing flame and the hot metal was just enough, to my blunted sight, to touch the walls, but I could make out a figure taller than myself picking its way across the littered floor with a confidence that I later realized indicated that he had waited outside until his eyes were attuned to the dark. By the wicket in the sliding door, which serves a second function by lining up with the door to the house when the big door is slid open, a second figure was standing, just a darker shadow in the deep gloom. This man, I suppose, had just switched off the lights.

It was a moment filled with extreme menace not yet relieved by action. I felt fear melting my stomach and legs, and an urge to panic and run; but I learned years ago, in many hard ways, to keep my head and think calmly in any emergency.

A battery powered inspection lamp was near my left hand, and I could have flooded the garage with light, but much of my married life was spent in the States in the days of the big gang wars, and a precept of my first husband came back to me. 'Never see their faces,' he would say. 'If you've seen their faces, they'll kill you. If you haven't, they may let you live.'

Instead, my fingers closed on an oddly shaped crowbar that Beau had picked up among a job lot of tools from someone selling up. We had never divined the purpose for which it had been made, and it was known in the family as the Thing for Taking Stones out of Girl Guides' Hooves. It felt as if it might also take the head off a hoodlum.

Adequately armed, I waited.

The moving figure paused, two paces away. The welding flame pointed at his face may have had something to do with his hesitation . . .

'What the hell do you want?' I asked. My voice sounded high.

A voice came from the nearer form, a calm, neutral voice without any of the local accent or any other, just a slight gruffness. 'You've been a naughty old girl,' he said, as if speaking to a bothersome child. 'We've come to give you a little reminder to keep your long nose out of other people's business . . .'

The tall oxygen cylinder was beside him. I could just make out the confident movement as he lifted his hand and shut off the supply. The dumpy bottle of propane was under the bench and out of his reach.

The other man started to slide the big door round to close the garage.

The man who had turned off the oxygen regretted his action within about three seconds. As the oxygen pressure dropped, so the flame turned from blue to yellow and stretched like an out-thrust spear, longer and longer. I had had no time to think, to resolve whether I could bring myself to burn a man who had not yet hurt me, and if the flame had been pointing away from him I do not think that I could have turned it his way. But it was pointing at his face, and I did not move my hand. For a second the scene was brightly lit and I saw the nearer man's face, long and thin and without compassion, heavy lids over narrow eyes, teeth bared and uneven, all under a head of straight, oily hair. Then the flame reached him, drew a red band up his face and past one eye into the oily hair before breaking into a short, smoking flare. I snapped it off and dropped it on the floor.

The man was yelling, in fear and pain and because his oily hair was crackling with its own little flames. I jumped forward and swung the Thing for Taking Stones out of Girl Guides' Hooves. It landed only a glancing blow, but it was enough to put him down, yelling louder than ever.

The blackness was utter, but I thought that the brief flare must have left them as blind as I was, and I knew the litter of hard and heavy objects far better, I hoped, than they did.

The other man, so far unsinged, was coming towards us. I heard him trip on an oil drum, step in the bath of paraffin, and crack some portion of himself on the corner of the big lathe – I recognized the sounds, for I had followed the same path myself. I slipped round the other side, dodged a trestle, stepped over the pump of the dynamometer, nearly got lost but oriented myself by the chains of the hanging tackle, and made for the door to the house. My foot landed loudly on a box of bolts, and I heard the man turn and move towards me, via the paraffin tray and the oil drum. I made a dart for it, found the big door and fumbled along it for the wicket.

Behind me, a foot crunched among the bolts, and then hands thumped the door beside me.

I found the wicket and tried to dive through, but, because he had started to slide the door, I bounced off solid brickwork behind.

An outstretched hand brushed my face.

With desperate strength, I swung the Thing for Taking Stones out of Girl Guides' Hooves, and it landed with a solid thump that was music to my ears.

That was enough. I scuttled for the big doors, tripped on a prone figure, stepped in the paraffin bath, and ran, banging my hip on the corner of the big lathe.

And then I was outside. It was as black as the tomb. I had expected starlight at least, or the reflected lights of the town two miles away, but this was one of those nights that are truly black. It must have clouded over while I pottered. I ran on to gravel, and on to grass which could have been either side of the drive or the small round lawn in the middle, and on to gravel again, and grass again and then more gravel. This was impossible if I were following anything like a straight line, but I thought that I must be proceeding generally away from the house.

There was no sound behind me.

I smelt metal and oil, and seconds later I walked into the side of a car.

This put a new factor into the equation. Hitherto, I had been concentrating my energy and my somewhat scattered wits on getting the hell out of the area and then making loud noises directed at Inspector Plummer in particular or, if he should prove unavailable or heedless, at the police in general. However, access to the enemy's transport was something else again. I could have wrecked it, of course, or immobilized it with something stuffed firmly up its exhaust – but I rather felt that anything detaining my new playmates in the vicinity was to be considered inadvisable. On the other hand, if I could lurk under a bush until they had driven off, and then phone the police to look out for a car with a . . .

With a what?

Looking back, I can see that I should have reached under a wheel arch and pulled the wire off a sidelight, but it is only too easy to be wise in retrospect. The weight of the Thing for Taking Stones out of Girl Guides' Hooves was still pulling at my fingers, directing my attention away from the electrics towards something more mechanical. And a broken exhaust would be detectable from a long way off – even by Inspector Plummer, I told myself.

I went down on my knees, felt under the side of the car, and found the round, dirty bulk of a silencer.

No more than a minute later, I knew that the Thing was not for Taking Stones out of Girl Guides' Hooves. It was a most efficient Thing for Taking Silencers off Other People's Cars. I hid the silencer under a bush that I found by walking into it, and tried to tiptoe a long way away, and quickly, despite the handicap that the shoe which had trodden in the paraffin was beginning to disintegrate. I had made some noise in my operations with the car, and unless the two men were lying unconscious in the garage one or both were hunting in silence. And to judge from their entry into the garage both were blessed with night vision much superior to my own. If I had known where I was, I would have headed for the kitchen garden, looking for a raw carrot to chew on. Instead, I headed for where I thought the road must lie.

When I was quite sure that I was near the bottom of the drive, I walked into a wall, and while I was still struggling to reconcile this irreconcilable fact the first crack of thunder from the overcharged clouds came, overlapping a brilliant flash of lightning. I was facing the wall of the house, beside the front door.

My back was to the open, and I saw nobody. But some-body must have seen me. Before the roll of thunder had died away I was gripped from behind and helpless, an arm imprisoning both of mine and a hand on my throat.

'I got 'er,' my captor called softly, and his voice was not the first one that I had heard but higher pitched and with a faint twang. 'You come quiet, missis.'

Coming quiet, I also quietly dropped the Thing on the grass. If I was not going to get a chance to use it, then nobody was going to use it on me . . .

I was frogmarched for ten yards, then stopped and held while hands, sure of their movements despite the dark-ness, took the scarf off my neck and tied it tightly round my eyes. Then they each took one of my wrists and led me, none too gently, over gravel and on to concrete, and I knew from the smell of oil and metal and paint that we were back in the garage. Faintly, through the scarf, I saw a wavering light spring on, and then steady, and I heard a torch being laid on the shelf.

'Over 'ere,' the second voice said tersely, and I was jerked round and pushed back to the bench. My hands were dragged behind me, and before I could guess what was happening the fingers of both my hands were in the jaws of the big vice and it was closed firmly. Two of my knuckles were trapped, and pain flamed up my arms.

'Tighter,' said the first man's voice. 'She can pull out o' that.'

'No,' I said desperately, 'I swear I can't.' The words came out almost as a scream.

A hand slapped me, casually. 'If 'e says you can, you can. Don' argue. Open yer mouth.'

I opened my mouth, but to scream. I was too late. A cloth, oily, from the bench, was forced between my teeth and secured by three or four turns of insulating tape right round my head. And the vice was given another part turn.

I stood still, and concentrated on tolerating the pain. There was nothing else I could do. I was gripped by fear, and yet I felt relief. There was no action that I could take except to submit. My range of choice and therefore of worry was strictly circumscribed. Thus, I was absolved of responsibility for what might happen to my poor clay.

Body warmth and silence told me that the two men were still standing in front of me, and I knew somehow, as one does, that they were looking at me, relishing my helplessness.

The second man, with the higher pitched voice, spoke first. 'I reckon that's enough,' he said. 'We don't 'ave to work 'er over.'

The other man sounded less dispassionate than before. 'Look at me bloody face,' he said.

'Not too much, we were told. Just a reminder. An' she's 'ad that. 'Ell, she 'it me too. What d'yer expect?'

'Yeah.' I heard the faint shadow of a laugh. 'It's what they call a love–hate relationship. I could bash her, but I take my hat off to her. She's got guts. I could almost fancy her, given half a chance.'

'No you couldn't,' the higher voice said uneasily. 'Christ, she's old enough to be yer ma.'

'But beautifully preserved, if a shade on the plump side. Still, I suppose . . .'

There was another silence, made hideous by not being able to see or speak, and by knowing that the man I had burned was considering whether to hurt me, and how.

I heard him grunt as he stooped, then my heart seemed to fall through the void where my stomach used to be as I heard him fumble with the oxygen cylinder. A match was struck on the wall, and the welding flame popped, spluttered and then settled to its small, venomous hiss.

I waited, braced for almost anything. Just as long as it wasn't my face . . .

At last it came. The flame passed across the almost bared toes of my right foot, as they protruded from the disintegrating shoe.

Beau, returning unexpectedly, found me the following noon.

Six

'I've had a wire from Jackie,' Beau said. 'She's flying
back again.'

I sat propped against pillows where I could look out of
the window at what I could see of the hospital garden. In
little more than twenty-four hours the English summer had
reverted to type. A blustering wind was flicking rain against
streaming windows, while under low clouds the light was
grey-white and sick looking, as if there were snow to come.
My head was still swimming slightly with the after-effects
of anaesthesia.

'Is she?' I said thickly.

'John'll bring the boat back. He'll be home in a couple
of days.'

'They didn't have to do that,' I said.

'What did you expect? She is your daughter, after all.'

'Not worth the trouble,' I grumbled. 'I've been hurt worse.'

'Oh? Such as when?'

'Such as before you were born, my boy. I remember
lying on the track at Brooklands with an ERA on top of
me, and there was a Bugatti on top of the ERA. That hurt
a lot worse.'

'I didn't know you'd driven an ERA,' he said curiously.

'I didn't,' I said. 'I'd been driving the Bugatti. Fanny
Birchell was in the ERA. It wasn't so bad when she got
down from the heap,' I added maliciously. Fanny Birchell
has not lost any weight in the last thirty years.

Inspector Plummer shifted uneasily in his hard hospital chair. 'Can we get back to more immediate happenings?' he asked plaintively.

'I've just told you all about it for the second time.'

'Yes, you have. And,' he said, 'I think you're playing it down. You make it sound like a picnic, and I'll bet it was anything but that. But now I want a description of the men – everything you can remember. Yesterday, you were so doped that you described about nine different people, most of them fit for a freak show.'

'Did I? I'll try to do better this time.' I paused, and collected my thoughts. 'One of them was above my height, about five nine or five ten, with a wiry sort of build and a long face like a goat. His teeth have gaps, or else they're badly crooked – I couldn't tell which – and he has protuberant eyelids, I suppose what you'd call 'hooded'. His voice was deep and scratchy, yet he sounded adequately educated. Not public school, yet no regional accent and a good vocabulary. He seemed to be the leader, and he was certainly the more aggressive. Vicious. Possibly sadistic. He has a burn up the left side of his face; and he used to have a lot of straight, dark, oily hair, but he'll have lost most of that and probably an eyebrow as well. I think he had light coloured trousers, but the rest of his clothes were dark.'

'That's much better,' Inspector Plummer said. 'Anything else?'

'Nothing. I only saw him for an instant, a rather hectic instant.'

'Go on. You're doing fine.'

'Well, the other one was more roughly spoken, with a higher pitch, and he had an accent that was either Cockney or Australian. I never saw him at all, but he was about my height – five feet four – broad, and muscular under a layer of fat. He'll have some bruises on him, and he trod in the tray of paraffin, so if one of his shoes isn't coming to pieces it'll certainly be affected. He was wearing something rough, maybe tweed. He was the more hesitant partner.'

'And that's all you can remember?'

'Yes . . . No,' I corrected myself. 'He'd smoked a cigar not long before, quite a good one. I smelled it on his fingers.'

'Got all that?' the inspector asked. The WPC nodded over her notebook. 'Well done,' he said, and I wondered whether he was speaking to me or to the policewoman.

'The taller one, the one who burned me,' I said, 'he seemed familiar with welding plant. And they both seemed to have far better night vision than I have.'

'They probably waited outside for their eyes to adjust,' Beau said. 'And, of course, you'd been welding. But they meant to grab you in the dark, or they'd have been wearing stocking masks.'

'Just as well for one of them that he wasn't. Otherwise, he'd have had melted nylon down the side of his face.' I said this with a certain amount of feeling. The removal of melted nylon from my foot had been a business which I shall take a long time to forget. 'Did I mention that they were wearing gloves?'

'Several times,' said the inspector. 'It explains the lack of prints, although it doesn't of itself mean that they were professionals. These days . . .'

'Would professionals have worn masks?'

He shrugged. 'Not necessarily. Not if they meant to attack and leave in the dark. Well, these are better descriptions than we usually get, although we can't do much more than consult other forces and circulate the descriptions. Of course, if they're pros and work as a team they may be easier to identify.'

'You think they're professionals? Hirelings?'

The inspector hesitated, then admitted that he did.

'Let me put it another way,' Beau said. 'Do you recognize them from the descriptions?'

'Yes,' Inspector Plummer said reluctantly.

'Who?' I asked, too quickly.

He shook his head sadly. 'I'm not telling you that, Lady P. Firstly because it might compromise a later identification, but secondly and more important because I wouldn't put it beyond you to hire some hoods yourself for purposes of retaliation, and I wouldn't like that.'

I yawned. The drugs were still working on me. 'At least,' I said, 'you can find out whether James Henshel ever had anyone answering those descriptions working for him, or in contact with him recently.'

Inspector Plummer swallowed nervously. 'You're serious?' he asked. 'When you said something like that yesterday I thought it was just the anaesthetic talking. Have you any evidence that Henshel was behind the attack? Did they let something slip?'

'No,' I said thoughtfully, 'they only said that they'd been sent to give me a reminder to keep my nose out of other people's business. I told you that.'

'So how do you figure Henshel?' Beau asked.

'I'll ask the questions, Mr Pepys,' the inspector said testily. 'Your aunt's quite entitled to have a relative present, or even a solicitor if she wants one, but I'll thank you to leave the questioning to me. Lady P, how do you figure – I mean, what makes you so sure that Mr Henshel was behind the incident?'

'Um,' I said. 'Beau, would you light me a cigarette and hold it for me? I don't want to set my bandages on fire. Inspector, I can only give you inferences, but I think they're strong ones. Just consider. Mac winked right at me just before he spoke to the foreman and got him to raise the question of cold storage. Ten minutes later you were accusing me of having put him up to it – which I didn't – and, the same evening, there I am pottering happily away and listening to "Sing Something Sinful", and I get attacked by men who say they've come to warn me to keep my nose out of other people's business.'

Inspector Plummer looked out of the window. 'I'm surprised it didn't occur to you that I might have sent them,' he said.

Occasionally, the inspector shows traces of a twisted sense of humour, but I can bandy backhanded insults with him any time. 'It did,' I said, 'but it doesn't conform with your known *modus operandi*.'

He looked back at me, sharply. I drew at the cigarette in Beau's hand, and blew a cloud of smoke at the ceiling. It was my first cigarette for two days. It made my head spin, but it was exquisite.

'You're assuming,' the inspector said, 'that Henshel was at the back of the whole business. You've no reason to believe that he had anything to do with Mrs Gallagher. There were plenty of other people at the inquest – including Bunt.'

'I may not have evidence,' I said, 'but I have reason. His plant handles dry ice and all kinds of gasses, so it must abound in freezing equipment. Have some fruit.'

'Thank you.' The inspector helped himself to a pear.

'Henshel sent me that basket of fruit,' I said. 'I hardly know the man, and it got here when the news of the attack was hardly out.'

The inspector swallowed a large mouthful of pear. 'That's no reason to take against the man. You're jumping to a whole row of conclusions,' he said. 'Because of your theory that she was frozen. Your mind's been affected by the anaesthetic. It's most likely that she just went away for a few months, abroad even, and came back just before her death.'

'And nobody saw her?'

'As far as we know. But it happens.'

'And no passport record?'

'That happens, too,' he said doggedly.

'If I might say something,' Beau began.

'Please do,' the inspector said, 'provided only that it introduces a fragment of reason, instead of all this half-baked conclusion-jumping.'

'Thank you,' Beau said. He put the cigarette between my lips, and left it there. 'Aunt, you must try to get out of the habit of thinking that because you dislike somebody that person must be guilty of something. It's not worthy of the scientific mind. Even if he is guilty, you're only being right for the wrong reason. Look at it the other way round. If he's guilty and you dislike him, then you have a bonus – you can actually enjoy despising him. Or you can dislike him because he's guilty. But your way round is a *non sequitur*.'

I had been unable to interrupt without dropping my cigarette down the front of my nightdress, but I could bear it no longer. I blew the cigarette out of my mouth on to the floor, where the inspector trod on it for me, picked it up, and deposited it in the ashtray.

'If you're quite finished,' I said, 'this much we are all agreed upon. The only visible reason for the attack on me is that I am believed – thanks to you and your loud voice, Inspector – to have focused attention on the time element and the possibility of the body having been dead all winter. And this in turn indicates that the instigator knew Molly Gallagher last autumn, has ready access to cold storage, and has the contacts to call in hoods whenever he needs them. And, to me, that spells Henshel. Damn it all, the whole affair smells of gas. I'll give him back his fruit one of these days,' I added grimly.

'Even if your line of argument's valid,' Inspector

Plummer said despairingly, 'Henshel is not the only person to fit your theory. It's easy to hire thugs. Just go to the right pub, put a few feelers out. That's all. We'll enquire, I promise you. We'll do everything in our power. I don't like hoodlum tactics on my patch. But I don't promise to let you know the result.' He hesitated, and then went on, slowly. 'There is one thing you don't know, which supports your argument as far as the inquest and the reason for the attack are concerned. Your friend MacKillop's here.'

'Of course he is,' I said stupidly. 'He works here. I'd like to see him later.'

'You can't see him yet,' Inspector Plummer said gently. 'He's in bed. He was beaten up, the same night that you were.'

I looked down at my bandaged hands, so useless on the blankets. 'Poor Mac. And he only wanted to show that he'd done his homework. It was the same men?'

'We don't know. He's still unconscious.'

I had to break a long silence. 'Beau,' I said hoarsely, 'bring me a handkerchief. I want to blow my nose. You'll have to hold it for me.'

Gently, Beau wiped my eyes.

Before he left, the inspector gently shook my right-hand bundle of bandage, a most unusual departure for him. 'When I arrived,' he said, 'there were two or three reporters trying again to get in to see you. I had them put into a waiting-room. Shall I send them packing?'

I sighed. 'I can't put them off indefinitely,' I said. 'Better to see them in here, where I've got all the resources of the National Health to eject them when I think they've had enough. Also, I'm in a position to demand sympathy. If I don't see them, they'll only make bricks without straw. What do you want me to say?'

'As little as possible, and nothing that connects up with Mrs Gallagher.'

'All right.'

'And I'll send a statement for your signature.'

'Do,' I said, 'if you think the courts will accept an X made with a pen held in my teeth.'

'Yes,' he said. 'Silly of me.' He went out, looking quite human.

Beau lit me another cigarette. 'If you'd had the dogs with you –' he began.

'A fat lot of use they'd have been. They'd probably have bitten me and licked the men's hands. And you know Solly can't stay in the same room with a welding flame.' I thought that Solly might be surprised to find me cowering beside him, next time the flame was lit.

'The inspector was right. You're taking it very calmly.' Beau was watching me closely, rightly suspecting, I think, that my calm was only skin-deep.

'What do you expect me to do?' I asked sharply. My fingers and toes were beginning to throb again. 'I'm in no fit state to dash about gibbering, and if my hands were ever in a suitable condition for wringing they aren't just now.'

Beau was smoking the cigarette himself, forgetting to offer me even a share of it. 'If it had been me,' he said, 'I'd be having a damned good shot at doing all those things. You could always rant a bit,' he suggested.

'I still can. But I'm told I did my cussing while I was coming out from the anaesthetic. Anyway, I'm still thoroughly tranquillized. I'll probably start yelling blue murder when it wears off.'

He grinned, uncertainly. 'That would be the day.'

'I hope you're not here to see it. Which reminds me. What brought you back so early? Not that I wasn't glad to see you, when you appeared so miraculously like the *deus* literally *ex machina*.'

He laughed, and relaxed a little. '*Ex machina* is just

about the right expression. After all the surgery we did before I left, the *machinum* – if that's the right word – seems to be showing symptoms of rejection, and it was convenient to call in at home to do a repeat operation.'

'Well, you do it,' I said, 'and then go finish your holiday. Don't hang around here for my benefit. I'm in this dump for about a fortnight, they tell me.'

'I happened to build this dump, in case you'd forgotten.'

'This very elegant hospital, then. You've worked hard all year for the sake of this holiday. Go and enjoy it.'

He started to protest, but we were interrupted by a small invasion of reporters anxious to know all about what one of them, a gauche youth from the local rag, referred to as the 'dastardly and sadistic outrage'. I gave them a short account of the events, without embellishment and omitting all reference to Mrs Gallagher and the inquest, and I denied having any idea of a possible motive for the attack. The reporters seemed particularly interested in Beau's timely return home to my deliverance, but then he is a better known figure to readers than I am. All in all, it was disappointing material, and they were soon filing out again – all but one. He, representative of a national daily, ducked back in as the door closed, a small but stout man with bright eyes. I remembered that he had served for a while as a science correspondent.

'One more question,' he said, 'and then I'll leave you in peace. Nobody thought to ask you what you were doing in the garage late at night.'

'You did,' I said. 'But you just didn't want to ask in front of the others.'

'Of course not. I am right, aren't I? The name nearly threw me, but you design under your first husband's name. Callender? Correct?'

'Perfectly,' I said.

'And so, what were you doing in the garage?'

A freelance designer can always do with a little publicity, but it must never be crackpot. 'I was starting to make the first prototype of a new system for medium and high speed petrol engines,' I explained. 'It will be a means of controlling precisely and automatically all the variables in relation to each other and to load, temperature and so on. But it's only in the embryo stage at the moment.'

Beau sat up suddenly. 'If there's anything in it from my point of view,' he said, 'this isn't for publication. And, Aunt, stop talking.'

I lay back in thought, and forgot my sundry aches. 'I shouldn't think so. It'll work all right, but my best calculations are that the weight will be too much, and the power gain too slight, to give any improvement in the power to weight ratio of a car except at the ends of the scale. Although, of course, the gain in fuel economy might make it worthwhile in long-distance races. I think its value, if it has any, will be where the performance demands are variable but weight isn't an important factor.'

The reporter raised a quizzical eyebrow. 'I wouldn't have thought there was much left to do for the petrol engine,' he said.

'You know better than that,' I said. 'You used to write a science column which was better informed than most. You know that the petrol engine hasn't had a quarter of the development that economic factors have forced in the case of the diesel. It isn't anywhere near its potential in efficiency.'

'Can you make it compete economically with the diesel? Keep smell off the roads?'

'I shouldn't think so for a minute,' I said. 'It's a good headline, but don't use it on my account.'

He chuckled, and got up. 'You designed the Warmaire

heating system, didn't you? I have one in my house. Works a treat.'

'Always nice to meet a fan,' I said.

When he had gone, prophesying that the local boys would kick themselves for not checking on their subjects, I gave my attention to my nephew. 'It's been nice seeing you,' I said, 'and I'm duly grateful for the timely rescue, but now go and finish your holiday.'

He hesitated, and just an instant too long. 'I think I'll stick around,' he said. 'Naturally, I'm concerned about you. I've had a very good run already, and in the other race meetings I'm entered for the competition's too hot for me. And, frankly, even if I can get the parts the car may take some time to fix without your magic touch.'

When Beau says 'Frankly', he's lying. 'That load of flannel,' I said, 'fails to convince me by a mile. You may be curious about this case, but you're not curious enough to forgo almost half of your annual tour. No. You've seen my hospitalization as a heaven-sent opportunity to install some young lady – for I give you both the benefit of considerable doubt – in the house. Permissive I may be, Beau, but I am not that damn permissive. I have never yet lived under a red lamp and I'm not going to start now. When you want an illicit honeymoon, be a man and face up to the motel costs. So go and finish your holiday, Beau, and go now. Your "mistress still the open road, and the bright eyes of danger". Stevenson wrote that before you were born, but he might have had you in mind.'

The house belongs to Beau, but he did not make an argument out of it. When you grant an aunt the status of an honorary mother, you must expect a little maternal interference along with the tender loving care. Any time that Beau feels that he has too much of either, he has only to say so and I will leave him in peace; and I dare say that his racing activities might still continue if, due to the expense of maintaining a separate establishment, I found myself unable to continue certain 'concealed subsidies'. So he just sighed, and got to his feet.

'I must be running along,' he said. 'I have a small removal to attend to.'

The door of my small room opened softly in the wee hours.

I was lying awake, resorting to my usual soporific of applying Bernoulli's equation, in my head, to the sails of various yachts, but without success.

The click of the latch made me start, and I turned my head quickly.

'It's all right,' came a whisper.

I was not convinced. 'Who is it?' I said loudly, feeling for the call button.

'Night sister,' said a normal voice, and the dim night-light came on. Sister Poole was just inside the door. 'Sorry,' she said, 'I didn't mean to startle you, but the light shouldn't have been out.'

'Well, you startled hell out of me,' I said. 'I thought they'd come to do me over again. But it's my own fault – I blustered the poor girl into switching the light off. What is it, Sister?'

'It's Mr MacKillop,' she said uncertainly. 'I believe he's a friend of yours?'

'Yes. An old friend.' I sat up. 'Is something wrong?'

'He's coming round, and he seems very distressed. He's said "Ladyship" several times, and we thought he meant you.'

'He probably does. Do you want me to come, or would I upset him?' I held up my bandaged hands.

'Would you? The house surgeon thought it might help. I brought your coat, and if you slipped it on and kept your hands in your pockets . . .'

She passed a comb through my hair, and we trotted down a warm, quiet corridor through a smell of suffering and hope to a unit which I recognized, with a sinking heart, as being for Intensive Care. At the threshold, I tried to cancel out my limp and buried my hands deep in my pockets.

Mac looked very old, very small, and almost dead, grey against the white sheets. A police constable, almost lost in a corner, was brooding over his open notebook. Beside Mac's head, a nurse stood still. Sister placed me where the bruised side of my face was hidden.

Mac stirred, turning his head from side to side. He moaned, a sound that sent a shiver up my spine and into the roots of my hair. And then, quite distinctly, he said, 'Ladyship.'

'I'm here, Mac,' I said. I had to clear my throat to get the words to come out.

I thought, at first, that there was too little of him left to respond. Then his eyes opened, turned slowly and tiredly towards me, and laboured to come into focus. A voice, weak and childish, said 'Ye're all right then?'

'I'm fine, Mac,' I said. 'Just fine,' while the middle finger of my right hand sent me a message that I was a liar.

'The good Lord be thanked,' he said on a windy breath. His accent was as strong as his voice was weak, and I knew then that, far from cultivating it as I had suspected, he must have spent years struggling to modify the accent of his youth. 'They said they was gaein' after ye.'

The constable was scribbling, and at the same time jerking his head at me, telling me to dig for the rest of the story. Sister Poole nodded, reluctantly.

'Who said that, Mac?' I asked.

'I dinna' ken. There was twa', and I didna' see either of them.' His voice was hardly even a whisper.

'What happened?' And when there was silence I asked again. 'What happened, Mac?'

'I misremember. I mind it was dark. And it was outside the house, and I was hit and went doon. I thought I was dead, but that I could still hear. And a voice said to tell *you* to keep out of other folks' business. I tried to speak but I couldna', and another voice said "Dinna' fash yersel', we'll away an' tell her ourselves",' Mac finished improbably.

'Anything else at all?'

'Yon's all that I can remember,' he said.

The constable tapped his watch. 'What time was this?' I asked.

'I don't know. Lord, but I'm fine pleased to see you're not hurt.' His faint voice trembled and then found a new strength, a touch of the old Mac. 'I know damned fine who was behind it, and if they'd touched you I'd've fixed him. He's not the only one as can play rough, and there's a few Glasgow lads of my acquaintance . . .'

'None of that, now, Mac,' I said hastily. His topic was interesting, but the law was listening too.

'Mebbe not,' he said. 'Just give me your hand a minute, so's I know it's really yourself.'

I looked up in horror, and met the sister's wavering eye. The young nurse kept her head. She beckoned me forward, and as I bent over the bed she stooped behind me and slipped one of her own hands into Mac's frail old paw. 'I'm glad you're all right,' he whispered.

There was a silence, and I quaked in case he should look down and see my bandages. Sister stepped briskly into the breach. 'You'll have to leave now,' she said firmly. 'I can't have the patient getting excited.'

'Go away tae hell,' Mac said with sudden force. 'My age, it'd take more than you and her together holding my hands to get me excited. Now, if it was yon wee nurse . . .' His head settled to one side as consciousness ebbed again.

The blushing nurse recovered her fingers from his importunate grip.

Seven

Jackie arrived next day bearing flowers, more fruit, wine and cigarettes, and shedding tears for no very obvious reason. She also brought a large posy of the day's papers, with accounts of my assault ranging in treatment from 'Dastardly Assault on Dowager' to 'Inventress Attacked' – the latter with a strong hint that I was about to revolutionize the transportation of the world. I gave Jackie a very toned down version of the events, and was able to assure her that Mac was now out of danger. I then spent an uncomfortable thirty minutes listening to Jackie, who declined to believe my theory as to the motive behind the attack. It was, she said, beyond credence that a lady should be beaten up because a man had winked at her – although she admitted that the converse might occur – and she was sure that I must have done something, and, whatever it was, I wasn't to do it again. Jackie, I fear, is turning into the sort of mother who will smack her child for nearly being struck by lightning.

I was too oppressed by the thought of having a real enemy to take kindly to filial nagging, and so greeted Beau with relief as well as pleasure when he arrived bringing – bless him! – more cigarettes, a long holder, and a very big lighter designed, I think, for the use of cripples. 'You have yet another visitor,' he said. 'Could you bear to see Alan Bunt?'

'Why not?' I asked, surprised. 'Alan Bunt, as far as we

knew, was the last man to see Mrs Gallagher alive. This could be interesting. And just supposing he was returning to the scene of the crime – me –'

Beau looked dubious. 'He's had at least a pint of lager.' Jackie sniffed. I remembered she disliked him.

I also remembered Alan Bunt's susceptibility to alcohol. 'He isn't obstreperous, is he?'

'Oh no. Very intense and well-meaning, or pretending to be anyway, but with something on his mind. He's anxious to see you, and bearing rich gifts. I went round by St Maggie's to see if the yard had any problems and to make arrangements about wages, and he came out of the pub and asked me to bring him here and arrange an audience.'

'I don't see many faces,' I said. 'Bring him in.'

'I'll be going,' said Jackie abruptly, picking up her bag. 'I've got a house to get in order.'

'Did you bring Tootles back with you?' I asked.

'Edward – your grandson – is with the Timmonses.'

'Give him my love, and don't forget to boil your hands before you pick him up,' I said. And then, relenting from my childish resentment at her attitude to my friendly if informal relationship with her son, I added, 'Are you using John's car?'

'I can't. He's got the keys.'

'Use mine while I'm in here.'

'Don't bother,' Beau said quickly. 'I'll jiggle the ignition on John's car for her.'

'Don't be silly,' I said. 'Let her use mine.'

'She can't, not without being arrested. I moved it into the garage, and it nearly deafened me.'

I lay back on the pillows and closed my eyes. 'You'll find the silencer under a bush,' I said weakly.

'Which bush?'

'If I knew which bush, I'd tell you,' I said.

Alan Bunt, when Beau brought him in, was walking

with the dignified care that only too much to drink can bring. 'Sorry,' he said. 'So sorry to hear. Terrible thing. Brought this. Said I'd buy you one back. Last chance.' And he produced a bottle of dry sherry, as well as some more fruit.

'Why, thank you,' I said. 'That's a very kind thought.'

He looked past my left shoulder at nothing. 'Fellow feeling. Happened to me once.'

I looked at Beau, and he was looking at me.

'It's not a very nice experience, is it?' I said casually.

He agreed that it was not, and then sat there looking at me.

'You must have a glass of your sherry,' I said firmly, and although he protested while Beau filled two teacups and a plastic toothmug he accepted a cup and drank, at Beau's suggestion, to my quick recovery.

'Our own fault,' he said suddenly. 'Needs careful handling.'

'What does?' Beau asked.

'*He* does,' Alan said. Beau's expression flickered.

'Of course he does,' I said. 'I just didn't think he'd go so far, did you?'

'No. Mistake. Been careful since. Soon won't matter.'

'We . . . you *are* both talking about the same person?' Beau asked.

Alan winked. 'Indispubitably,' he said, taking care over each precious syllable.

I devoted an urgent second to wondering just how I could ask the right question to find out if he was telling the truth – or feeding me a red herring. 'We're on the right lines, are we?' I asked.

He winked again. 'Getting warm,' he said. I was to think, later, what a singularly inappropriate expression that was.

A direct question might have scared him off the subject. 'Go on,' I said.

Alan Bunt shook his head. He tried to lay his finger along his nose, but missed it by several inches.

'All right,' I said. 'But why did you get the treatment?'

'Didn't handle him right. Unnerestimated. But out of evil cometh thingummybob, though I've watched step since. He's ruthless, Lady P. Ruthless.'

'Is he indeed,' I said. Who was he talking about – himself, or Henshel or a third party? 'Beau, pour my guest another sherry.'

Alan sat while Beau refilled his cup, his wavering eyes on or around me in a look of concern, but never able to actually meet mine. 'No more,' he said thickly. 'Careful now. Soon won't matter. But tell you this.' He leaned forward until I thought he was going to fall on his face, and lowered his voice. 'If you have any more bother, or think he's maybe sending 'em after you again, tell 'm you've got the tape. Just tell 'm that.'

'The tape? Recording tape?' I guessed.

He nodded, several times.

'Recording of what?'

'Jus' me 'n' him.'

'That will stop him?'

He smiled, in silence.

I would need time to fit this fragment of advice into the pattern, but I knew that it would fit somewhere and that time would bring the explanation. 'But you have the tape, of course?' I said.

He laughed. 'There isn't any tape. Never was. But he doesn't know that. Couldn't see it.'

'Who couldn't see what?' I asked despairingly.

Alan Bunt sipped his drink in silence, but Beau was inspired. 'If I remember from my visit to your office, you kept your dictation machine on a shelf below your desk, didn't you, Alan? So, of course, one couldn't see whether it was running or not.'

Alan nodded again, proudly. 'She knew it was bust, though.'

'Who's she?' I asked. 'You mean Mrs—?'

He got to his feet and swayed. 'Said enough. Too much, in fac'.'

'Oh dear!' I said mildly. 'Beau, I think you'd better drive him back again.'

Alan waved the service aside. As I watched, he was turning a greenish white. 'Doesn' matter,' he said. 'Soon be gone. Never meet again.' And he opened the door and walked into the wardrobe.

'Hurry, Beau,' I said. 'I think he's showing symptoms of rejection too.'

Within a week I could use my right hand again after a fashion, and I resumed my work on the design sketches immediately so that, by the time I was at last released from hospital, every detail of the first prototype was clear in my mind and on paper. By that time, Mac was on the road to recovery, his continued improvement being evidenced by a fury that mounted steadily and dated from the day he was told that I too had been a victim.

And while I worked my subconscious turned over the following facts: Alan Bunt had accused someone, whom I took to be Henshel. Perhaps they'd had a falling out – I could check whether Bunt *had* been beaten up. But maybe this was Bunt's revenge – to frame Henshel? The inspector could be right. I was allowing Mac's hatred of Henshel to colour my own thinking. And what did Bunt mean this was the last we'd see of him?

Beau drove me home, over roads that steamed in a new sun. 'I think it must have rained throughout my incarceration,' I said.

He grunted, negatively. 'Perhaps it just feels that way.'

'Maybe. No disrespect to your *magnum opus*, Beau, but it's lovely to be out in the world again.'

He took his eyes off the road for no more than an instant, to look at me in warning. 'Remember, you'll have to take it easy.'

'Or what?'

'I don't know what,' he said grumpily. 'Or you'll do yourself an injury, I suppose. I'm only going by what the doctors said.'

'Well, you and Jackie had better come down to earth,' I said. 'If I were fool enough to try to sit still and do nothing, I'd go mad in a couple of days and end up doing everybody an injury.' I tapped the fat envelope on my knee. 'Know what this is?'

'They gave you the deeds of the hospital for good behaviour?'

'Say a little prayer tonight,' I advised him. 'Pray that every morning you may wake up slightly less of a twit than you were the night before. No, these are letters.'

'Sympathy?' A car in front was throwing up mud. Beau slowed and used his washers.

'Not exactly. Nibbles. That bit in the papers . . .'

'Ah,' he said absently. 'Manufacturers not wanting to miss out if it turns out to be good, and oil companies wanting to have control of any fuel economy devices?'

'Mostly,' I said, 'yes. But one more interesting one. A speculator through a dummy, and I know something about the dummy, the intermediary. What makes it really interesting is that while I think I may cause a little interest in academic circles I honestly don't think that any commercial application's going to emerge. With diesel priced as it is, most of the heavy users would be better to stay diesel. Small cars couldn't carry the extra weight or cost, and with most of the other users – boats and aircraft, for instance – loads are so steady that self-adjusting fine tuning's unnecessary.'

'Keep plugging on,' Beau said. 'You usually manage to find a silver lining somewhere.'

'This time, it's for the people who sell me materials.'

'And gasses?'

'Don't remind me,' I said.

In Downfield High Street, I asked Beau to stop.

Inspector Plummer's visits to me in hospital had been devoted mainly to assertions that he was following all lines of enquiry but had not found my attackers yet, and to long accounts of the work he was planning and doing on *Dawn Breeze* with frequent requests for technical advice; but I had persuaded him to obtain for me the necessary papers, and I now found to my surprise that the gunsmiths were able to sell me an automatic pistol over the counter.

Depression was a new companion for me. Usually, if I am depressed, I am too busy to notice it. Yet now my morale was low and my mind seemed to search for depressive or nostalgic meanings in the most trivial incidents.

I was determined not to give way to fear; on the other hand I was touched when the family, sensing or anticipating the fears I hid so carefully, conspired to see that I never had to leave the house or return to it alone. During the working week this put a load on Jackie, yet she found a succession of ingenious and light-hearted excuses for accompanying me here and there.

Often, of course, I was alone at home, and then the pistol was a source of comfort to me. I never tried to wear it in a holster, although my figure is better contrived for the concealment of firearms than that of, say, Modesty Blaise, although I say it myself. When out of the house it came along, quite illegally, in a large handbag; indoors, I carried it in my hand or laid it down beside me. Thus it was readily available for the repulsion of intruders, but liable to be a source of embarrassment in the event of

unexpected guests. I tried to pass it off as a novel but un-
reliable cigarette lighter until the occasion when I poured
tea for an old friend and looked up to see her on the point
of blowing her stupid head off. The family took to singing
loudly as they approached the house.

On another occasion I took the thing outdoors and fired
it. It threw straight enough but, apart from being disappointed at the unimpressive noise – for I had been
expecting 'the cannon's opening roar' – I considered it a
poorly engineered device. The action felt wrong, and it
stung my hand with burned powder. Later, I locked myself
in, took the thing to pieces and designed a modification
which is now standard and which earns for me an annual
royalty which almost pays the television licence.

The dogs surprised me by being another source of
comfort. Usually either dormant or else either aggressive
or friendly but always each with the wrong people, when
their long noses smelled my fear and the general concern
they turned from dim-witted pets into slightly dangerous
guards. As Beau had suggested, I kept them with me, and
it took only an unfamiliar footfall or the slam of a strange
car door to raise their savage voices in great snarls that
made the hair crawl on my neck and stopped the visitor
in his tracks. The postman stopped delivering to the door,
but stayed in his van and sounded the horn until I came
out for the mail. I was only vulnerable to the butcher, who,
fortunately, was as good a friend of mine as he was of the
dogs. I kept as a close secret the fact that they were terrified of guns – that an assassin with a cap-pistol could have
sent them packing in a hurry.

Those dogs were more sensitive to my fear than I was,
for their nervous state lasted when I was sure that I had
forgotten if not forgiven . . .

Late in July, six weeks after my release from hospital,
I was working in the garage as usual. The house was

empty, the dogs were leashed to the bench, and the gun was on the shelf.

A bloodcurdling growl from Cressida drowned the approaching engine, but I heard a vehicle's door slam, round at the front of the house. I silenced the beasts, and called, 'Who's there?'

There was no answer. The dogs exploded again.

That was enough for me. I took down the pistol, and unchained the dogs. When I heard footsteps outside, I let them go and they flicked out of sight.

I waited, limbs shaking. From where I was, the visitor would be silhouetted against the half open doors if he survived that far. To judge from the noise, he was being torn into gobbets.

Yet a shadow fell across the door. A dumpy figure in cap and dungarees entered the doorway, carrying in either hand a dumpy gas cylinder, and I recognized one of the drivers from Henshel's firm. Around his legs the dogs raged, threatening terrible things, their noise a high-pitched yell redolent of bloodlust. Only the man's extraordinary air of immunity was deterring them from attacking.

The man trotted placidly in, looking me blandly in the eyes. I had the gun behind my back, and I slipped the safety-catch. He might be a brave man, but one false move was going to earn him a series of punctures along a line from his trachea to his pelvis, inclusive, followed by a crack over the head with the empty pistol if he was still twitching.

He put down the cylinders, and pulled the empties out into the middle of the floor. Sol, suspecting mischief, feinted at his hand with a snap like a rat-trap, and was ignored. The man produced his delivery book and offered me a pencil.

And, as I tried to ask if he hadn't brought me oxygen as well, he turned his hearing-aid on.

I have never seen so quick and complete a change in a man since the day a hired Santa touched a faulty fairy light, on Jackie's third Christmas. As the appalling menace of the dogs at last reached his poor ears, he was transformed on the instant from a placid, middle-aged man going peaceably about his employer's business into the victim of a thousand terrors. I had barely time to see his face change before he took off in a backward, twisting leap that carried him six feet towards the doors, and he was running before he landed.

He might as well have tried to outrun an arrow or one of my bullets, for a Borzoi can run down a fleeing stag. The dogs were after him instantly, quite beyond my control and going for a kill.

There was just one action open to me which would avert bloodshed and litigation, and God inspired me to think of it in time. I lifted the pistol and pulled the trigger.

Even I was startled by the resultant noise. The report, which had seemed a feeble pop out of doors, boomed in the close quarters like a cannonade, while the bullet, passing through a light-fitting tube and all, glanced off a steel beam, ricocheted again off the big lathe – which rang like a gong – and left by way of the window.

The dogs raised their voices an octave and, with an incredible burst of acceleration, overtook the man on either side and passed out through the doors together. The man, seeing his enemies before him, tried to brake sharply on the very spot where my sump usually drips oil, skidded and fell heavily.

The noise of the dogs died away, and the garage was filled with a low moaning and the stench of cordite.

Mr Thorne – this turned out to be my visitor's name – was pacified eventually by nine cups of strong tea, a small whisky and a very full explanation of the work I was doing in the garage. In this last he seemed remarkably interested and well informed. I had the impression that he had been primed with some special questions to ask, so I primed him in my turn with some special answers. But again, if he was snooping on Henshel's behalf, the man was only being a good businessman. Thorne left at last, promising forgiveness, and I was out with Beau until midnight, recovering the dogs.

Eight

It was a long, fine summer, but I saw very little of it. I sailed with Jackie and John a couple of times, and I attended the British Grand Prix with Beau, who failed to qualify, but my mind was not on the events and I was always glad to get back to work. I was in the grip of my special project, and became too preoccupied to concern myself with even the interesting demise of Mrs Gallagher.

The prototype was assembled, tested, modified, tested again, partially redesigned and remade, and the final version still showed points open to improvement. However, in the early autumn I published the data in a carefully worded article in the *New Scientist*.

That article brought the vultures down on me again, as it was calculated to do. Teams descended on me, each including an accountant and an engineer. I knew most of the engineers. Some of them clearly agreed with my view of the economic prospects, and from those I heard no more, but I received several offers, always on a royalty basis. The situation was confused by the fact that there were now two speculators in the field, each acting through a second party, but, as I had suspected, the approach made to me while I was still in hospital proved to be through a lawyer employed by a subsidiary of National Fire Defences. He uttered one of the figures which I had implanted in the unfortunate Mr Thorne, and I sold him the entire research outright. I received his cheque on the spot.

That evening, I took Mac out for a meal, in celebration and, in part, compensation. Henshel had tried to bully Mac once, and now I felt the score was settled when he would undoubtedly lose money on my new invention. I also wanted to believe he was responsible for both Mac's and my injuries – Mac was sure of it, but I knew I must not let my judgement be clouded by his old feud. The jury was still out, there were many unanswered questions. And, I noticed, Bunt had indeed disappeared. Sailed *Grey Goose* right out of our lives. Now why?

I awoke next morning to the unfamiliar and uncomfortable sensation of having nothing to do. During the busy summer the domestic strength had been enlarged by the usual expedient of asking our cleaner if she could extend her hours, and she was coping admirably. I had no great urge to resume domestic chores just yet.

It was a glorious autumn day, cooler but with a perfect little breeze stirring the browning leaves and just visible as a ruffle on the water, so I took the dogs and walked down to Jackie in the hope of arranging a sail.

Jackie gave me a cup of coffee and a cigarette while she finished swabbing my grandson down. 'I don't fancy your chances for a sail,' she said brightly. '*Queen Aholibah*'s away on a late charter, with Dave skippering. The rest are mostly laying up just now, so John's got his hands full. I'm going over shortly to help out in the office, so if you want to go and try you can give me a lift.'

'You don't just want me to come to babysit?' I asked suspiciously.

'I don't know that I'd trust you.'

'Hard words, but that's how I like it. Although I've nothing to be absent-minded about just now.'

'You'll think of something,' she said.

I took the dogs home and collected the car. Toots sat

on Jackie's knee and put the lights and wiper on and off, sounded the horn, switched the radio from channel to channel and finally removed the choke from the dashboard by the roots. We were all a little fractious by the time St Maggie's was reached.

A new row of parking meters had appeared in Hill Street, so I turned the corner and found a space in front of the Rose and Compass. Jackie was making for the yard office to relieve John and I told her to tell her Lord and Master that I would be over shortly to see if he wanted a hand with anything. And I occupied myself until she was out of sight in switching off the lights and trying to fit the choke cable back. Then I dived into the bar. I always feel a little dehydrated during the unwinding process that follows a bout of work, and Jeremy's bar in mid morning is a haven of peace in which to think quiet thoughts.

I must have ruminated there for half an hour or more, for I was on my third Bacardi-and-lime when Jeremy put the telephone in front of me. 'Ladyship, your nephew wants you.'

'It rang?'

He nodded.

'I didn't hear it,' I said. 'Hello, Beau.'

'Hello again, Aunt. I've been trying to reach you. I called the yard, and Jackie said you were probably—'

'Well, I am,' I said.

'No reason why you shouldn't be. Are you still interested in the Gallagher business?'

'I'm just beginning to recover my interest,' I said. 'Why?'

'Well, I happened on something this morning that might shed a little light. I think. I took my dictation machine into the specialist shop that sells them, and also does repairs, because the wind-back had stopped winding back, and I saw a dusty-looking one on the shelf that looked just like the one Alan Bunt used to use. I remember it because it had an unusual cream and red case, not the usual battleship grey. So I chatted awhile with the assistant.'

'And could the young lady tell you anything?' I asked. 'About the dusty machine, I mean, not your blue eyes.'

He cleared his throat. 'The subject of my eyes did crop up, as a matter of fact. But, almost as interesting, it *was* his machine all right. I suppose that with him and Mrs Gallagher both leaving nobody knew where it was, or even cared that it existed. It was brought in for repairs, by Mrs Gallagher, on – guess when – no other than October the eighth last year. The girl showed me the ticket.'

'That's the day—'

'The day Mrs Gallagher was last at work,' said Beau. 'Quite so. But my informant after a little prodding – purely oral, or I should say verbal, I assure you – remembered something else. Your friend Henshel was collecting something of his own when Molly Gallagher came in, and seemed very interested in the fact that it was broken. He left with her.'

I made a silent whistle. 'You have used your charm to good effect.'

'Does it fit in anywhere?'

'Your charm?'

'I know very well where my charm fits in, thank you, Aunt. I meant the information, as you very well knew.'

'My dear boy,' I said, 'it goes plink into place, three raspberries fall in line, bells ring, lights flash, a recorded voice cries "Bingo" and a shower of sixpences come down the chute. I was just sitting and hypothesizing a series of events into which that fits very neatly.'

'Ah. Well, no doubt you'll tell me all about it tonight.'

'If you've been good,' I said.

He asked me to put Jeremy back on. Jeremy listened for a few seconds, and then hung up. 'He says not to give you any more,' he said.

I emptied my glass and pushed it across. 'Fill it up again,' I said firmly.

I pondered halfway through my last drink. A part of the pattern was showing, but, it was like a jigsaw puzzle in which the background was developing but the main items just would not fit together. However, one strong theory was starting to clarify. I borrowed the telephone and called Mac at his home. Our conversation was guarded, but he was quick on the uptake.

Then I went out, into the crisp day.

As Jackie had said, there was no prospect of a sail. The few boats still in the water were for the most part already stripped of their masts. Several trolleys waited at the bottom of the slip for the tide to rise and a few boats were standing by, waiting for enough water to get on to the trolleys. Another boat, under the crane, was being dismasted amid cries of anguish and fatuous advice. The harbour had lost its gay summer look of being thronged with dormant but purposeful boats and was taking on its lonely winter aspect, when only the utilitarian workboats would sit on its waters.

The lack of sailing I could bear philosophically. The breeze had died and it was a dead flat calm.

Jackie and John were in conference at the gates of the boatyard, but broke off as I approached them.

'Morning, John,' I said. 'Anything I can help with today?'

He shook his head. 'Later, perhaps,' he said. 'Just at the moment, no . . . Unless you'd like to keep Ray Plummer out of my hair for a while. He wants some advice about *Dawn Breeze*.'

'Ah,' I said. 'He is here, then. I thought I saw his car. I want to see him anyway. By the way, whatever happened to Alan Bunt and *Grey Goose*? I'd've liked to talk to him as well.'

Jackie made a face. 'He's somewhere around the Canary Islands by now.'

'Is he indeed?' I said.

'And we're well rid of him,' she added.

John sighed. 'I still can't make out what you've got against him,' he said.

'He's a thief,' Jackie said bluntly.

'Oh, come now—'

'He is,' she persisted. She turned to me. 'You know what it's like trying to convince a man that his friend's no good. It's the biggest closed shop in the world. But that man Bunt has sticky fingers. You know how easily things walk around a harbour.'

'Are you sure?' I asked, puzzled. This didn't accord with my new and precious theories.

'Sure? Of course I'm sure, Mother. There was rather a nice winch which went missing from the yard, and it turned up on *Grey Goose*, repainted but recognizable. After that I kept an eye on him, and several other bits of gear found their way on to *Grey Goose*.'

John scuffed his feet and looked up at the sky. 'I gave him that stuff,' he said at last.

Jackie stared at him. 'Are you just trying to alibi your little pal, because I seem to remember that you acted very mystified when that gear disappeared. Was that an act?'

John waved his hands, helplessly. 'I'm afraid it was. Maybe I was unnecessarily surreptitious, but I was sure you wouldn't approve.'

'But why?' Jackie asked plaintively. 'Why, for God's sake? We're a business, not a Benevolent Society.'

'I felt sorry for him. I thought he was – OK.'

'You think nearly all the men around here are OK. And every woman in her teens and twenties. But you still haggle like a carpet seller, and sulk if you haven't squeezed the last penny out of a deal, just as a matter of pride. So what got into you? Why the special relationship?'

John flushed. 'I didn't fancy him, if that's what you mean,' he said defiantly.

'I know that – who better? Don't be silly.'

'You wouldn't understand.'

'Try me.'

John had started to turn away, but he faced Jackie again. His jaw, never exactly receding, jutted, but he was clearly embarrassed as well as determined. He looked like a caveman caught with his tiger skin down. 'Alan had very little money,' he said. 'He was scraping the bottom of the barrel. But he'd got out of the rat race, and before he got back into it again, as he knew he'd have to do some day, he wanted to do what any . . . well, he wanted to do a circumnavigation.'

'The world? Right round?'

'Yes. Taking his time, two or three years, and alone. He said once that after a trip like that he'd be able to face the prospect of going back to work and being sweated until he was too old to be happy any more.'

'It is possible to be happy though aged,' I said, but they ignored me.

'But . . . but we knew nothing of this,' Jackie said.

'You didn't. He kept it as secret as he could. He didn't want any fanfares.'

'And I'd have broadcast his secret?'

'I didn't say that.'

Jackie frowned. 'Even so, why should you want to contribute?'

'I thought he'd had a raw deal.'

'Was that all?'

John hesitated, and then rushed on. 'Damn it, I'd sell my soul to do that trip myself.'

There was a shocked silence.

'It's out of the question,' Jackie said shakily. 'Put it out of your tiny mind.'

'I did,' John said. He spoke very gently. 'I may not be very bright, but I know when I'm trapped.'

Jackie flinched at the word. 'Toots and I couldn't come with you. How could we leave everything?'

'We couldn't,' he said patiently.

'Even if you went alone, what would we use for money?'

'I don't know.'

'Everything we have's locked up in the yard. I couldn't run it for that long by myself. It's out of the question.'

John turned his back. 'I know it's out of the bloody question,' he said, over his shoulder. 'I've told myself that over and over again. That's why I wanted Alan Bunt to go. Maybe I would only be going vicariously. But even I can have a dream.'

I coughed as tactful a cough as I could manage. 'I'll go and see Inspector Plummer,' I said. As I went I thought, what seemed cut and dried was as clear as mud again.

The inspector was looking younger and happier than I had ever seen him. He was walking around *Dawn Breeze*, squinting up at a tracery of mast and rigging and the framework of a new cabin and doghouse which, I could see, were beautifully laminated out of thin strips of teak.

'You are getting on,' I said.

He patted her stern complacently, and smiled at me. I gathered that we were sweethearts again. 'Not bad,' he said. 'I'm almost ready to put the decking on. But before I commit myself that far I wanted to be sure I hadn't made it too high. It gives splendid headroom inside, but I don't want to make her top-heavy.'

I studied her new outline. 'No,' I said. 'No danger of that. The extra windage may lose you a little speed to windward, but only a little.'

'Will the boom have enough clearance over the hatch? I don't want it to take my head off some time.'

'It'll come a bit higher when the sail's set.'

'How much, d'you think?'

'Why not set it,' I suggested. 'It's calm enough.' As casually as that are the seeds of great disasters sown.

'Good idea. If I set the jib at the same time I can mark the positions for the doohickeys that the sheets run through.'

'Fairleads,' I said patiently.

He hopped up the ladder, happy as a schoolboy at the prospect of playing with his toys, and fished up his sailbags from under the foredeck.

I hesitated, and then spoke up. My theories were only theories and they could never be anything else unless I took the plunge and used the inspector to fill in the gaps. Unfortunately, the gaps might be filled in with facts that I would rather remained unknown, but I decided that in Alan Bunt's absence I could afford to take the chance.

'Have you closed your file on Mrs Gallagher?' I asked.

'That file will never close,' he said, without any particular emotion. 'No evidence. No witnesses. Not even a credible theory. Nothing.'

'I'm beginning to get the first faint shadow of a theory,' I said. 'It doesn't help with the death or reappearance yet, but some odd bits of information that I've picked up add together to explain her presence in St Maggie's and why she might have been of importance at the time. Of course, I've very little evidence –'

He broke off from lacing the mainsail's foot, and looked down at me. 'Never mind that,' he said. 'It's my business to get the evidence, and I have the facilities to get it – once I know what I'm looking for. So let's have your theories.'

'Right,' I said, mounting the ladder. 'I'll come up with

you, so that I don't have to shout. And while I'm here I may as well lace the head for you. Now . . .

'Let's start from what my nephew told us. Alan Bunt, as acting county architect, had authorized a lot of work by the gas installation contractor, and had been led to believe, rightly or wrongly, that he was going to be left to foot the bill.

'Who would he contact?'

'Don't ask rhetorical questions. It's your story. Tell it, if you must.' But the inspector leaned his elbows on the boom and waited.

'Henshel, of course,' I said. 'Not only as the contractor concerned but also as a county councillor and a known fixer. After all, Henshel would have to see that the account was paid by the county if he was to get his money. Alan Bunt doesn't have that sort of cash, and any court in the country would have given him about a hundred years to pay. Or so Alan Bunt would have reasoned.'

'Sounds quite logical so far.' He stirred, and started tying off the end of the lacing.

'I think so. But I think Mr Bunt was getting out of his class and pitting himself against a much keener and less scrupulous mind. Probably anyone but Henshel, in the same circumstances, would have said "Nonsense, Deevie – Mr Devlin – can't do that. Legally, he's bound to settle the bill even if he wants your head on a salver afterwards." And if he'd said that, I don't think any of this would have happened. But, Henshel being Henshel, he wouldn't do that. From what I hear, he's never been known to pass up a chance to play both ends against the middle. So what would he do?'

'I see what you mean. He'd suggest—' The inspector broke off, and gave me one of his rare grins. 'Damn. You nearly caught me there, you and your rhetorical questions. You carry on, but give me a hand hoisting.'

I took the throat halliard. 'Henshel would undoubtedly exploit the situation by proposing a fiddle.'

'What sort of a fiddle?' He squinted against the sun.

'At a guess, he'd suggest that he wouldn't submit the extra account at all, it being settled instead, with bonus, by the back door – I mean by some overpayment on the original contract and by having future work steered his way with his own assistance in committee and then being overpaid on that.

'So far, I must admit, it's pretty assumptive. But I think you'll find the assumption supported by the evidence that comes up for the next steps. Alan Bunt, in his cups, told me that if I had any more trouble with Henshel – and, mark this well, we were talking about assault by hired toughs – just to tell Henshel that I had "the tape", and he admitted that he was talking about a recording that never actually existed. That, he said, would stop him. He also added that "he" – Henshel – "couldn't tell it was bust". Now, my nephew tells me that Alan kept a dictation machine down behind his desk, and it was bust. So we can gather that Henshel made some such corrupt proposal.

'Alan Bunt, I'm assured, isn't as dim-witted as his manner perhaps led Henshel to believe, and he would certainly see that once he accepted any such proposal he'd be pretty much in Henshel's power. So he put up a bluff. He pretended that his machine had been working and that he had a tape which he'd take to the council or to the police. If there was any backlash.

'Shortly thereafter he says was beaten up in the street – you'd have records on that, wouldn't you – presumably by hirelings looking for the tape, or just to give him a lesson. Perhaps his office and his digs were searched at the same time? Nothing was found, of course, because the dictation machine had been taken for repair. Result, *impasse*. Bunt, scared to make any move, throws up his job. Henshel, not sure if there's a tape, is unwilling to present the extra account until he's sure, just in case it stirs up the mud. And Devlin is quite prepared to settle the account if it's presented, but quite happy if it isn't.'

Inspector Plummer finished snapping on the staysail hanks and moved back to the halliard. 'Anything else?'

'Oh yes,' I said. 'Plenty. You see, Mrs Gallagher took the machine in to the agents for repair. Not immediately, or she might be alive today. Eventually she took it in for repair, not realizing that it had any significance, and Henshel happened to be there in the shop and was very interested. He left with her, very curious, of course, as to just when the machine went wrong. My nephew got this today from the assistant who served them.'

'Hum!' the inspector said. 'He'd testify?'

'She,' I said. 'I gather so.'

'Well, it's a start of sorts. What happened then?'

We climbed down the ladder, and looked back up. The sails glowed softly in the bright sunlight. 'You've plenty of clearance over the hatch,' I said. 'And you want the foresail fairlead at the bottom of the third frame back. Sheet it there for the moment and mark the place.'

He started back up the ladder. I let him get to the top before I spoke on. If he was going to fall on his head, he could do it while I wasn't talking to him.

'This took place,' I said, 'on the eighth of October. That's the day she disappeared,' I reminded him.

He finished a knot before he spoke, and then he said, 'Aha! Is that the lot now?'

'For the moment. I've got to do some more research before I can take it any further. But there's one thing that ought to be done first.'

'The dictation machine? It's still in the agent's shop?'

'It was this morning.'

'And it might still have a tape in it . . .'

'It might,' I said, 'although it's unlikely that there would be anything worthwhile on it. But I think you ought to get on the phone.'

He came down the ladder and looked at me as if he was wondering whether to give me a short course in egg sucking. 'I don't have to use the phone,' he said, 'I can use my car radio.' And he ducked into his car. Apparently the inspector was taking me seriously. For once.

I could see my son-in-law down by the harbourmaster's office, and I walked along to join him. John was looking chastened but defiant, his dream still intact.

'John, could your records show what the harbour was like on eighth October last year?' I asked. 'What boats were away, which were still in the water and which were hauled out? Also, if possible, which boats were out on their moorings and which were alongside.'

John gave me a look that said, almost as plainly as words, that if I hadn't been principal shareholder in his business he would have invited me to jump in the harbour. 'Not very easily,' he said. 'I suppose I might be able to cook up something between my diary, the office records and the harbourmaster's books. My accounts may help. And *Queen Aholibah*'s logbook. I hope it isn't urgent . . . When d'you want it?'

'Yesterday or the day before. It's urgent, John, urgent. Don't let Jackie delay you,' I added, as she appeared, with Toots in tow.

Jackie looked white and resolute. She marched up to John as might a Christian martyr approach the smallest lion in sight, determined to get it over as soon as possible. 'If you want to go,' she said, 'go.'

'Go?'

'Yes, go. Round the world,' she explained.

'Oh, there.' John came out of his reverie. 'It's out of the question. We agreed that.'

Jackie stamped her foot. 'Go, damn you, if you want to so much.'

'No,' John said. He stalked off towards his office, his footsteps booming on the heavy timbers. 'I can't,' he called back.

Jackie blew her nose.

Nine

Inspector Plummer slipped out of his car as I returned. 'Here goes another of my rare days off,' he said, but he said it happily. 'I'll expect you to help me with the boat to make up for the time you're costing me.'

'I gather there was a tape?'

'There was and there is. A car's gone to collect it, but they played it to me over the phone. The last message was to Mrs Gallagher, instructing her to make an appointment for Mr Henshel to see Mr Bunt.' He looked at me benignly. 'And the agent's records confirm that Henshel was in their shop that day, collecting a mini recording device.'

Instead of being pleased at this sudden if partial confirmation of my hypothesis, I felt a spasm of trepidation. I was in danger of being stampeded into the next stage of argument, and I was unready for it.

'If you're right so far,' he said, 'and it looks as if you may well be, then Mr Henshel was quizzing Mrs Gallagher as to when the machine went phut, or whatever it went. Would she appreciate the significance of the questions?'

'Possibly. Even if Alan Bunt hadn't primed her, she'd have had to be pretty dim not to guess that the subject was important. Probably Henshel overestimated her loyalty to the county and underestimated her loyalty to her ex-boss, and came straight out with his questions.

Whether she knew why he wanted to know or not, she would have seen that her answer must be significant to both men. She shook Henshel off and went back to the office, but she must have made up her mind to come over to St Maggie's as soon as she clocked off, to see Alan Bunt.'

'To assure him of her loyalty, do you think?' the inspector asked.

'Or to tell him to run for cover. Or possibly to see if her new importance was worth anything in cash or kind. We won't know until we can ask Alan Bunt – and he's sailed over the horizon, quite conveniently.'

'With Henshel hot on her trail?' The inspector was not to be diverted by thoughts of Bunt.

'Possibly,' I said. 'Possibly.'

'Last October . . .'

At that point, we were interrupted by the clangorous arrival alongside *Dawn Breeze* of a large, throbbing vehicle, emblazoned with the insignia of National Fire Defences Ltd. My friend Mr Thorne hopped down from the high cab. He approached the inspector, turning up his hearing-aid as he came. ''Ere,' he said firmly. 'What you doin' with Mr 'Enshel's boat?'

'It's my boat now,' said the inspector.

'That's Mr 'Enshel's boat, that is,' Mr Thorne persisted. 'Been delivering to it for years. I got me orders.'

I hushed the inspector's impassioned defence of his title to *Dawn Breeze* and stepped in front of him. I had a tingle up my spine. The hour produces the man, and Mr Thorne had been of unwitting service to me once before . . . 'What orders have you got?' I asked.

He hesitated, and then decided that the information was unclassified. 'October until end of March, alternate Wednesdays, dry ice,' he said.

How wrong, I thought, he was. In forgetting to cancel

138

that standing order, Henshel had made a mistake that he would regret, and bitterly.

The inspector pushed past me. 'Dry ice? To *Dawn Breeze*?'

Thorne nodded.

'What for?'

'Dunno.'

'I can guess,' I said. 'It would saturate the atmosphere inside the boat with carbon dioxide. Dry rot, inspector, thrives in oxygen. Of course, it would need a well-sealed cover.'

Mr Thorne was nodding happily. ''At's right. I 'ad to lift a tarpaulin an' a sheet of plastic, and afterwards tape the plastic down again and tie the cover.'

'And,' I said, 'it would keep the whole boat cold. In a long, cold winter like last one it'd be like a refrigerator most of the time. What time of day did you deliver usually?'

'Any time. Whenever it suited.'

'Could you tell what time you delivered here on the eighth of October last year?' I asked.

He nodded. 'I could. If I did. But why should I?'

'You know who I am?' the inspector asked.

Mr Thorne smiled faintly.

'Well, I want to know. That's why you should tell.'

Thorne shrugged. 'I got to go back to the depot for more bottled butane. I can look it up in the office.'

'You look it up and come back and tell me. And do it without making a song and dance about it. One more thing – what did you deliver it into? I mean, you didn't just pour it into the boat. Did you leave the containers or what?'

''Ole in the deck, with a cover,' said Mr Thorne. 'Like a small man 'ole, I poured the gas in there. That all, then?'

'That's all for the moment.' The inspector watched him climb into the cab and reverse away, and then turned back to me. 'But . . . but that was his coal-locker. It still had an inch of coaldust in it.'

'It could have been coal-locker in the summer, dry ice box in winter,' I pointed out. 'That would be quite a sensible arrangement. Neither would contaminate the other.'

'I wondered why it was insulated.'

'Obviously, that's why. You'd better keep it carefully – it's another of our few pieces of evidence.'

The inspector closed his eyes and breathed heavily. 'I threw it away,' he said miserably. 'I was doing away with the stove and the damn locker was tucked in behind the heads, which stuck out into the companionway. I wanted to move it back out of the way.'

By an enormous effort of will I refrained from even smiling, let alone giving vent to the great gusts of laughter that were boiling up inside me. 'If you ever say another word to me on the subject of tampering with evidence, I will have the whole story printed and circulate copies around all the police forces of southern England. Could you get it back?'

'I suppose so. I dropped it in the harbour.'

'Naughty,' I commented. 'You are in a jam, aren't you. If you use frogmen the police will know what a brick you dropped and the harbourmaster will get on to you for depositing rubbish in his beloved water. You'd better borrow John's big magnet and fish for it after dark.'

Inspector Plummer frowned. Pride demanded that he contradict me. 'If I need to.' He closed his eyes and leaned against *Dawn Breeze*'s rudder. 'Let's accept as a reasonable working supposition that Mrs Gallagher came over to St Margaret's, looking for Mr Bunt. Let's also accept for the moment, that she could have been gassed on board *Dawn Breeze* when Mr Thorne delivered the gas. And let's even accept as another possibility – subject to expert advice

– that a body laid up in an insulated boat, in cold weather, and frozen fortnightly by the juxtaposition of a large quantity of dry ice, would keep until spring, we still have a couple of serious gaps in the story. Why was she on *Dawn Breeze* at all? And how did she come to be found on your son-in-law's boat instead?'

I only half-heard his last words because I had been thinking furiously, partly along those very lines. The rest of the puzzle was beginning to fit together, but there were several pieces that could fit in different ways.

And I wanted them to fit my way. The trouble was likely to be lack of evidence, and yet shortage of evidence might be on my side. I had an uncomfortable feeling that no matter how I manipulated the facts Alan Bunt was likely to come in for sharp scrutiny. Could he have deposited the unfortunate or even unconscious Mrs Gallagher on board *Dawn Breeze* to await the coming of the gas? If she had threatened him, he might have lashed out and then decided to frame Henshel. That was not a theory I liked.

'We need my son-in-law,' I said. 'If we know where the boats were at the crucial times we may have a chance of explaining both points.'

'That's easy enough. He's over there talking to Alan Bunt – who may be able to help us even more,' the inspector said grimly.

I said a very rude word, but I said it under my breath.

We met them by the harbourmaster's office just as Jackie, carrying Toots, came out of its door. 'I thought you'd gone out of my life for ever,' Jackie said. Her manner to Alan Bunt was friendlier.

He smiled sadly. 'I should have done.'

'Maybe you should, at that,' I said.

The inspector was bursting to speak to Alan Bunt, but Jackie was determined to have his attention. 'What brings you back?' she asked. 'I thought you were in the trade winds by now.'

'I had some rotten luck. I was out beyond the Scillies, trying to make south, when I sailed right on to something in the dark – a drifting buoy, I think. She was holed, just above the waterline. I got a patch of sorts over it, and made it back to Fowey. It took me two months to repair, because I had to do the work myself and I had to replace quite a few planks. And I was just about to start off again when I made a last check and found that my mast was sprung. I think she must've laid it against the quay at low tide while I was ashore.'

Inspector Plummer, who for all his few virtues has a one-track mind, was anxious to ask Alan about Mrs Gallagher's last hours; Alan was aching to ask John about masts; John wanted to get all the interesting technical details. Jackie was trying to get her oar in somewhere, but failing in the teeth of so much competition she turned to me, offering a handful of papers. 'This is the data you were asking John for,' she said, as the three men put their heads together.

'Good girl,' I said, accepting them. 'Now, do you think you could find out the date when Mr Henshel first came down to uncover *Dawn Breeze* and start the spring fit-out?'

She pursed her lips. 'I think so. It was just after that last cold snap, and he called in about ordering some paint. I booked the order, and it was probably date stamped.'

'Well, whatever date it was, find out where all the boats were from then on, for a couple of weeks.'

'Oh, no! Not again,' she said weakly.

'It's urgent, Jackie, and important.'

'It'll take ages.'

'It mustn't,' I said. 'You didn't take long last time.'

'I can't go on dropping everything else whenever you blow the whistle, Mother. What's it all about?'

'It's about Mrs Gallagher. Well, could you get me the relative movements of *Dawn Breeze, Grey Goose* and *Queen Aholibah*?'

'I suppose so.'

'And quickly?'

She looked at me speculatively. 'I could do it quicker if you looked after this lump for me . . .'

I was spared the painful necessity of refusing the proffered Toots by an interruption that stopped all our conversations in their several tracks and took our minds off trivialities such as death and babies.

A white squall came out of nowhere, a screaming blast of air that made us stagger. It whipped the gravel off the quay to sting our skins and rattle against the office. In the harbour, rigging sang wildly and boats rolled and plunged on their moorings. The group at the crane were in trouble, with a swinging mast still half inside a rolling hull, and John ran to help them.

Jackie yelled something and pointed, and we swung round, eyes screwed against the wind. *Dawn Breeze* was trundling towards us, a brave if horrifying sight with her white sails straining. The trolley groaned and swayed under her, but held a straight course. Behind, the tow-bar scraped a furrow in the quay, ploughing up more gravel to whirl towards us on the blast.

We ran to meet her – Alan Bunt, the inspector and I. Inspector Plummer was uttering prayers couched in terms of which I was sure the recipient would not approve.

Alan Bunt and the inspector met the boat ahead of me. The inspector grasped one of the supporting struts and threw all his considerable weight into a desperate attempt to restrain his rampageous pride and joy, but against the pull of about forty square yards of canvas taut to bursting point, he was as nothing.

Bunt's contribution was more practical. As the boat

came abreast of me, I saw that he had grabbed up the tow-bar and was steering her clear of the bollards. 'Do you think I have room to try and turn her upwind?' he gasped.

I didn't think so. The harbour wall was much narrower here, and the violent turn that would be required, if it were possible at all, would certainly topple her over. Better, I thought as I jogged along beside the strange vehicle, to continue as we were going. The harbourmaster's flimsy office might not stop her, but it would certainly slow her down before she hit the wall beyond.

And then, in horror, I saw that Jackie, with Toots still in her arms, was standing before the door of the office, probably seeking admission out of the wind or in search of the information I had just demanded. Her back was towards us.

'Head her round the harbour,' I yelled. Alan Bunt nodded as best he could and leaned on the bar. The whole crazy rig veered round, heeling over on the springs of the chassis and creaking ominously. A wedge dropped out, and I picked it up and ran after.

The wind was now abeam and she picked up speed, rumbling loudly as the wheels passed from the solid quay on to the heavy timber wharf. I spurted forward and banged the wedge back into place with the heel of my hand. The inspector had fallen back on the power of prayer again, so far without conspicuous result, and I felt that something more positive was required. We needed sail off before Alan was confronted with the alternatives of ploughing into John's yard with its cluster of expensive vessels laid up around it or launching her down the slip in the faint hope that she might emulate a lifeboat at the bottom and yet not sail herself to destruction against one of the harbour walls.

The group at the crane had forgotten their own problem

and were gaping at us with the concentration always reserved for other people's calamities . . .

Desperately, futilely, I ran beside the boat, jumped, grabbed the gunnel and got my feet on to the chassis below. And there I found myself stuck. I could not drop off again without risking falling under the wheel, and yet, with the chassis frame too far under the turn of the bilge to give me a purchase to jump from, my physique prevented me from hauling myself up and aboard.

The inspector seemed puffed. He was dropping behind, calling feebly on us to stop. If he had had breath to spare I think he would have added 'In the name of the Law'. Alan still steered grimly. I would have called on him for help, but if the boat had rounded up to windward I would have found myself in the water with the boat on top.

Feet rang on the timbers behind me, and I heard John's voice. 'Up you go,' he said, and gave me an upward push which in any other circumstances I would have resented bitterly. Then my head and torso were over the side-deck and I could grasp the bare frames for the new cabin. I rolled and scrambled to comparative safety, no doubt presenting an unedifying aspect of myself to the group by the crane as I did so, and fell over into the cockpit to avoid the rigging of the hanging mast which was blowing out towards me on the wind. The snap hook on a halliard missed scalping me by an inch and wound itself irredeemably around *Dawn Breeze*'s tiller. As we rolled majestically along, the halliard, of course, came taut. *Dawn Breeze* barely faltered, but the mast swung out on the crane's sling and bent, impossibly. Just before the hook snapped off the halliard I heard the sounds of disintegrating timber, and of voices raised in distress, but I had no time to stop and stare. Action had to be taken before worse befell.

The mainsheet was near my hand, and I cast it off. The boom went out against the running back-stays and she slowed slightly. We were at the inner corner of the harbour now, near John's yard, and I shouted to Alan to turn her again, and he swung the tow-bar.

I clambered forward, grateful for the handhold of the bare framework.

The turn had brought us up almost into the wind and with the mainsheet free she should have slowed, but the laws of nature seemed to have ceased working for us.

And I could do very little up for'ard. Inspector Plummer, in improvising mood, had used the tail of the peak halliard to sheet the clew of the foresail, and the wind was holding it out bar taut and beyond my reach. I threw off the fore-sail and throat halliards, but each sail only sagged a foot or two and jammed.

I looked up. We were rapidly approaching the top of the slip. That way might have lain salvation, but the water was still too shallow and there were boats and trolleys in the way.

I yelled to Alan again, and saw his teeth as he grimaced with the effort of turning her away from the harbour.

Then I saw why she had not slowed. Inspector Plummer had seized the trailing end of the mainsheet and was hanging on to it in a desperate attempt to slow our mad progress, but his efforts were serving only to pin the big sail in and increase its drive. This was not the inspector's day for brilliant ideas. Even as I realized what he was doing I saw John drag him away from his limpet grip, but the damage was done. We had made our turn, and the wind was back on the beam.

'John,' I shouted, 'throw me your knife.'

He nodded, and grabbed at his belt. A bare sheath knife cartwheeled up towards me. Not for anything would I have tried to catch that bare blade. I ducked aside and as it dropped between the frames I dived after it through the hole where the hatch would eventually be. The floor was up, and I saw the knife between two pigs of ballast. As I stooped and grabbed for it I saw something else, but had no time to pause and investigate.

As I heaved myself back into the cockpit again, trying to close my mind to the pain in my knees and the precariousness of my situation, I saw that we were already passing Jeremy's pub and entering Hill Street. I had come for a sail, but I had never expected to sail up Hill Street.

Ahead was a jam of traffic.

I cut the tackle of the running backstay, which let the boom go broad off and slowed us a little. Then I dashed for the mast. Overhead, the yard fetched down a festoon of telephone cables. The nearest bus was very near. In a fever, I slashed the peak halliard on both sides of the cleat.

There was a thunder of flogging canvas. The long yard dropped at last into the branches of a tree, breaking a streetlamp as it fell, and as I was buried under great folds of mildewy cotton I felt *Dawn Breeze* slow, halt and roll back to a stop against the kerb.

It seemed very peaceful, all of a sudden.

I struggled free, resisting the temptation to cut my way out. We were neatly parked, at four parking meters. 'I told you that was the best fairlead position,' I said.

Inspector Plummer panted at me.

'You'd better come down,' said John. 'It looks pretty unsafe. Most of the wedges are out. Come over the stern and I'll catch you.'

'Just coming,' I said. But before climbing down over the stern I made another trip down into the vestigial cabin to investigate the odd plastic object which I had noticed protruding from between the two pigs of ballast. It was quite stuck and I had only seen it at all because John's knife had landed almost on top of it.

Alan and the inspector were leaning, panting, against the chassis. A small crowd was collecting.

'What the hell do I do now?' Inspector Plummer asked the world at large.

'You could start by putting shillings in the meters,' John said, 'before a warden comes along.'

'There's a time for doing it yourself,' I said, 'and a time for leaving it to the professionals. This is the latter. I suggest you just instruct my son-in-law to get her back whence she came . . .'

'Yes,' said the inspector. 'Please.'

John nodded. I thought he looked a little dazed.

Jackie arrived on the scene. Toots was slung over her shoulder. He seemed to have slept through all the excitement. Jackie pushed through the bystanders and confronted John. 'We'll get a more suitable boat,' she said, 'and we'll go. The three of us.'

'I think I owe you a drink,' the inspector said to me. 'We'll be in the pub.' He took Alan Bunt by the cuff and led him away.

'We can't,' John said wearily. 'Who'd look after the yard?'

'Mother would,' said Jackie. 'Wouldn't you, Mother?'

'I've got a better idea,' I said firmly. 'You stay here, all of you. I'll go.'

'But—'

'But nothing,' I said. 'Go and find out those things I wanted to know and be quick about it.'

Ten

It was midday. The bar was crowded, and twittering with excitement over the recent spectacle.

There was no sign of the inspector, or of Alan Bunt, but the bell from the back room was ringing, and I saw Jeremy pick up a tray. I caught him by the door. 'Don't answer the bell,' I said urgently. 'Not unless it rings three times in a row.'

Jeremy just nodded. He can be very quick on the uptake.

'And when the inspector comes through,' I said, 'he'll ask for a special cocktail for me. I just want a Campari and bitter lemon, but take your time mixing it.'

In the back room the inspector, although still flushed and in a highly nervous state, seemed well aware of his honourable obligations. 'By George,' he said, 'you were splendid, both of you! I suppose you realize you saved me a lot of money?'

'We were aware of that,' I said.

'The least I can do is to buy you a drink.'

'The very least,' I agreed. 'Some of Jeremy's pâté sandwiches would go down well, too.'

'Now, wait a minute,' he said. Jeremy's pâté sandwiches are expensive.

'Or shall we claim salvage?' I asked Alan.

He looked interested. 'Can you claim salvage on a boat found in the street, abandoned and apparently doomed?' he asked.

'We could find out.'

The inspector's high colour left him. 'Sandwiches it is,' he said hurriedly. 'And beer?' He rang the bell again.

'I'll have one of Jeremy's special cocktails,' I said.

Alan asked for a small shandy.

'I'll go and get them myself,' the inspector said wearily. As soon as the door closed behind him I looked carefully around in case the room had a serving hatch that I had never noticed before. But we were quite safe from eavesdroppers.

'Now,' I said. 'Quickly, in case he makes Jeremy promise to bring the drinks and things through. Just confirm that I'm right, and trust me. Mrs Gallagher came to see you down at the harbour, the day she disappeared?'

He hesitated, looked away and nodded.

'You left her aboard *Dawn Breeze*, didn't you?'

He looked at me in dismay. 'What makes you—'

'We mayn't have time for that,' I barked at him. 'Did you or did you not?'

'Yes,' he said under his breath. 'God help me, yes, I did.'

'Alive and well?'

'Of course.'

'Don't bother to sound indignant. Just answer the questions. In the spring, you found her on *Grey Goose* – but not alive and well?'

'Yes.' His voice was faint.

'And moved her on to *Queen Aholibah*,' I said.

'I . . . I'm afraid so,' he said miserably. 'You see, *Queen Aholibah* was going abroad shortly afterwards, so I put her in there, in the aftercabin. I thought John might just – I don't know what I thought. I was desperate, I wanted to get away and I was afraid. I knew John would know what to do.'

'You might have known that John would report the dead

body to the police. Others might have thrown her in the Channel. But not John.'

'I was sure I wouldn't be believed. Not if certain . . . other things came out.' His hands trembled. He needed his drink.

'Well, they're out,' I said brutally. 'About Henshel and the contract and the tape. You can talk freely about that. But say nothing about having moved the body.'

'Say? I'm not saying anything to anybody,' he said sharply. 'I want to get away again, not drag around the courts for the next six months.'

'You're too late anyway. The hurricane season would be well established before you could get near the trade winds. Stay until spring, take a job with Beau, mend your tattered finances a bit and help me to fix Henshel.'

He shook his head roughly. 'I don't want to be within his reach. As soon as I can get another mast, I'm going.'

'We can fix him, I tell you.'

'No,' he said. 'No.'

I had been listening for the loose board in the passage to creak, and it did so now. I reached out and pulled the door open, hoping to find an embarrassed inspector tiptoeing to the keyhole, but Jackie came in. She dropped a sheet of paper in front of me. 'Here you are,' she said. 'It was easier than I thought.'

Quickly, I ran my eye down the neatly tabulated facts. It was as I had feared. I had not been at the harbour to witness Henshel's first visit in the spring, but on one of my own visits I had noticed that *Dawn Breeze*'s winter cocoon had been reduced to a few canvas covers. This had been in the first few warm days of the year, and only a week or so before *Queen Aholibah* sailed on her early cruise. My memory, which is quite often dependable, insisted that *Queen Aholibah* had been out on her mid-harbour mooring at that time, that *Grey Goose* was the only boat moored alongside, and that the few boats still ashore were secure inside the fence of John's yard. Jackie's notes confirmed that this had been the state of things when Henshel paid his first call.

'Thank you,' I said sadly, and I tucked the papers firmly away in my pocket. The yard's records would have to be expurgated before Inspector Plummer got near them, to hide the fact that Mrs Gallagher had rested briefly on *Grey Goose*.

'You can have the mast from *Anita*,' Jackie said. 'She was gunter-rigged until last year.'

Alan glowed. 'Can I really? Thank you, thank you,' he said in heartfelt fashion. There was no denying that the man was in a hurry to get out of the sphere of Henshel's influence. Well, it would take him a few days to rig and step a strange mast. Perhaps it was all for the best. If I wanted him again I could catch him, but it might well prove that his absence would be preferred to his company.

'Jackie,' I said, 'get the hell out of here.'

'I beg your pardon?'

'You heard me,' I said. 'Go and change Toots or something. In fact, I'll come with you. Alan, tell the inspector all about your squabble with Henshel. But don't go beyond the subject of the tape until I get back. Say nothing more. Got me?'

He said that he had indeed got me.

'Come, girl,' I said.

In the corridor, we met the inspector bearing a heaped tray. I took my drink up, drained it, and helped myself to a handful of sandwiches. 'I'll be back in a minute,' I said. 'I think I can get a little more evidence for you.'

'But—' he called after me. 'But—'

Outside, 'What was that about?' Jackie asked me plaintively.

'Partly,' I said, 'because those notes you brought me would have sent Alan Bunt up the river along with Mr Councillor Henshel. I was hoping all along that Henshel moved Mrs Gallagher on to *Grey Goose*, partly for convenience, but mostly out of spite. And Alan Bunt moved her again. He dumped her on you because you were going abroad. He just admitted as much to me. He sends his apologies. He's been misguided, driven into a corner – by Henshel.'

'Handsome,' said Jackie grimly. 'Can we believe him?'

'Calm down. He was in a tight spot and admires your husband's capabilities as much as you do. The thing is, I don't want you to give access to your records to Inspector Plummer until I give you the nod.'

'You mean, until you've done a little editing?'

'Jackie,' I said, 'what a thing to say to your own mother!'

I took a quick bite of sandwich. It was delicious.

The NFD Ltd lorry was pulsating away patiently outside John's yard gates, and I caught Mr Thorne as he emerged. His delivery to *Dawn Breeze* on the eighth of the previous October had been made during the evening, because of a factory fire in Downfield which had kept all vehicles running supplies of carbon dioxide to the fire-fighters during the day. Mr Thorne parted with this information with only token reluctance, but his eyes were becoming sharp with curiosity.

Jackie was lurking nearby, equally curious, and I turned to her as Mr Thorne rumbled away. 'Who else around here owed Henshel a grudge?' I asked quietly. 'Strictly between ourselves, of course.'

Jackie pondered. Obviously the question did not strike her as odd, but then Jackie, too, can be very devious when so inclined. 'Only Geoff Allen, that I can think of,' she said at last.

'And God alone knows where he is. Nobody else?'

153

Jackie laughed at me. 'He's been back here for the last three weeks.'

'Has he? I haven't seen his old tub,' I said.

'She's here.'

'I'm damned if I see her,' I said.

'Try looking for a blue boat. He's repainted her.'

And then I saw *Fidelity*, moored to the wall, fifty yards away. 'All right,' I said. 'So I'm blind. Thank you.'

I found Geoff down in the big cabin that was once the hold of the former inshore trawler which is now his home. Geoff looks every inch the sailor, but in fact he managed a bank until a few years ago when he lost his wife. As soon as the funeral was past Geoff sold his house, bought *Fidelity*, and moved aboard before even starting the necessary conversion. He now spent most of the summer cruising, eking out his slender income with occasional charters.

Geoff welcomed me aboard, sat me down and gave me a glass of duty free gin from his considerable stock. He is not a talkative man, so I could safely enquire after his recent trip – down the Portuguese coast and back, he told me – which formality past, I got down to business.

'You know Mr Henshel?'

His face, which had been serene, turned prunish. 'I know him,' he said.

'You like him, of course?'

'No.'

'Ah?'

'Look,' he said, 'last year I kept *Fidelity* over on the outer wall. Well, it's handy when you're living aboard – the tap and the electricity box are nearby. He used to bring *Dawn Breeze* alongside whenever he wanted to water up or to take gear on board. A lot of them did. I didn't mind. But I had to stop Henshel in the end, because he was careless with fenders, and he had sharp bolts on his chain plates which chewed up my topsides. I warned him often enough, but he just looked at me. So I told him to go somewhere else. Next time he came alongside, I wouldn't let him across my deck.'

'He wouldn't like that,' I said.

'He didn't.'

'So what did he do.'

'A few days later my new dinghy went adrift, and drifted along the wall. He charged *Dawn Breeze* straight at it and sank it. I tried to claim, but he maintained that he had crushed it accidentally while trying to salvage it. I couldn't afford to fight him.'

'Perhaps it's as well you didn't try,' I said.

'Perhaps it is,' he said.

'I want you to think back to last April, about the fourteenth or fifteenth. You were here?'

He fetched his log from the neat chart table between the wheelhouse and the cabin. 'I was here,' he said, with his finger on the page.

'About then, Henshel came down to *Dawn Breeze* for the first time in the year. He took off the winter coverings.'

'I remember that. I was on deck, doing some varnishing.'

'You saw him?' I said, pleasantly surprised. 'What happened?'

'Let me think . . . I was watching him, wondering if he'd ever stick his neck out for me to chop it.'

'And I think that's exactly what he did,' I said. 'Go on.'

'All of a sudden, you've made me very happy,' he said, with a faint smile. 'He came down in his car, and parked by the yard office while he went in. I presume he was buying something, or paying his account. Then he walked round the far side, to *Dawn Breeze*. He got his stepladder out of the shed, untied the covers and folded up the plastic sheeting and put it away in the shed. And then he did a slow and careful inspection of the hull.'

'Without going down into the cabin?'

'At that time, yes. He prodded around with a knife for a bit, and then . . . yes, he went aboard and down into the cabin.'

And got the shock of his life, I thought with pleasure. 'And then?'

Geoff shrugged. 'He was down below for some little time. Then he came out and covered her up again with the tarpaulins, well laced down. And he left.'

'How did he seem when he left?'

'Perhaps a little agitated, but it's hard to tell with him. I noticed that he seemed to be in a hurry, and yet he stopped and looked down into *Grey Goose*, which was alongside nearby. Then he walked quickly round the harbour, into his car, and drove off like the hammers of hell.'

I looked him straight in the eye, and spoke very softly. 'Not *Grey Goose*,' I said. 'Your memory's playing tricks with you. It was *Queen Aholibah* that was alongside there at the time.'

He swallowed that one in silence.

'You remember, of course,' I went on, 'that he came back that night, or possibly the next, after dark.'

I couldn't tell how much sense he was making out of what I was saying, but I saw the lines around his eyes crease in a faint show of inner amusement. 'Remind me,' he said.

I thought before I spoke. Anything too precise would be suspect, and would leave him open to being asked why he had not thought of taking his knowledge to the police.

'Of *course* you remember,' I said at last. 'You were sitting on deck, in the shadow of the wheelhouse, for reasons that I'll leave you to recall for yourself. You saw his car come down and park over by the pub. You recognized it because it was so large and quiet. A figure came walking round the side of the harbour. You couldn't see it clearly in the dark, but when it passed under that lamp on the corner you recognized Mr Henshel. You had the impression that he was looking around to see if there was anyone else about at the time. He walked, quickly but quietly, round to *Dawn Breeze*.'

Geoff nodded. 'What did he do then?'

'That's all that you saw,' I said reluctantly. This was as far as I dared manufacture evidence – at least by a single witness. But I was convinced I was right now and Henshel had to be trapped somehow. 'You went below after that. But it's important that you remember that *Queen Aholibah* was deserted at the time.'

'It's all coming back to me,' he said solemnly.

'One more thing,' I said. 'Don't be rash. If he isn't safely out of harm's way after you've told your tale, stay where his boys can't get at you.'

On my way back through Jeremy's bar, I collected another round of drinks as a peace-offering – with a pint of bitter for the inspector and a very weak shandy for Alan Bunt. If there was one tongue that I did not want babbling that afternoon it was Alan's.

In the back room, Inspector Plummer was liverish, and Alan was sweating nervously. 'The inspector was in a great hurry to discuss . . . how Mrs Gallagher came to be at St Maggie's.'

'But you didn't tell him?' I asked.

'No.'

The inspector accepted the drink, but spurned it as a peace-offering. 'Why didn't you want him to tell me the rest?' he demanded.

'Because I wanted the fun of telling you myself.'

'That sounds like you. And where did you rush off to just now?'

'I . . . got Mr Thorne's times from him,' I said.

'That wouldn't take so long. What else?'

I swallowed something that seemed to have lodged in my throat. I could hardly say that I had wanted to suppress some of Jackie's testimony. 'Geoff Allen's back in the harbour,' I said reluctantly. 'You remember, I mentioned him?'

'Yes.'

'He has a story that I think you ought to hear.'

The inspector was still suspicious, but only on general grounds. And he was in a hurry to get the rest of the story. 'I'll speak to him later,' he said. 'Meanwhile Mr Bunt here confirms your theory. I have to take off my hat to you, Lady P. Mr Henshel suggested a deal along the lines you suggested, and Mr Bunt threatened him with a non-existent recording of the discussion.'

'Aha!' I said. 'And then, Alan, your machine got sent for repair, and Henshel happened on it and guessed that it might not have been working at the crucial time. He tried to pump Mrs Gallagher, and she still had some loyalty to you. She came over to see you here. Right?'

Alan sighed. 'Yes. She said she'd have to tell him the truth. He'd been on the phone to her twice during the afternoon, and he was a councillor, and what could she do? But she'd come over to warn me first, bless her, because she'd guessed that it was something both important and damaging to me.

'I could see her problem, of course, and I just hadn't the resources to give her money to go away until the whole thing had blown over. So I could only see one chance for myself.

'The way I saw it, chucking up my job hadn't got Henshel off my back. I tried to convince myself that the interest in me that he'd shown to Mrs Gallagher was only because of his fear that the tape might exist, but I couldn't. He's not the type to forgive being thwarted, let alone bluffed. And it's an open secret that his little revenges aren't always very subtle.'

'Is that what it is, Inspector?' I asked. 'An open secret?'

He flushed. 'I've never had enough evidence to use in court,' he said. 'And,' he added very quietly, 'I've never had any encouragement from on high to go looking for any. But don't quote me on that.'

'I won't,' I said, 'but I'll remember that you said it. That man's not *compos mentis*. He's confusing himself with God.'

'Not an easy mistake to make,' Alan said. 'Anyway, I thought that if I could gain a little time while Henshel was still uncertain about the tape I could muster my arms. I thought that if I could team up with others of his enemies – and I could name several – I might be able to do a deal with him. My silence for my safety sort of thing.

'So I asked her to stay out of circulation for the evening. I hid her aboard *Dawn Breeze*, thinking he wouldn't look for her on his own boat. I borrowed her car and headed for Downfield to see what I could save from the wreckage.

'Unfortunately for me, Henshel must have been quite certain that the tape didn't exist. There was a welcoming committee at my house. They warned me against opening my big mouth, and then they gave me a beating that put me in hospital overnight. When I got back here next day *Dawn Breeze* had been bedded down for the winter and there was no sign of Mrs Gallagher, and no message from her either. Her landlady told me she hadn't returned – and when I went to where I'd left her car, it was gone. I decided she must have gone.'

'But why on *Dawn Breeze*?' the inspector asked. 'Why

not on your own boat? It was taking a big chance he wouldn't return.'

'It had to be *Dawn Breeze*,' I said. 'That much was a foregone conclusion. I've had my daughter raking through the records all day. It appears that Alan's boat was out on its moorings in the middle of the harbour. The only boat alongside was Geoff Allen's, and he was living aboard. *Dawn Breeze* had just been hauled out the previous day, and was laid up under covers. She was the only boat ashore not locked up behind John's yard fence. Even if Mrs Gallagher had fancied a trip out to *Grey Goose* in the dinghy, the tide . . .' I did a mental calculation back to the eighth of the previous October. The tides repeat themselves once a fortnight. '. . . The tide would have been right out,' I went on, 'and she'd have had twenty yards of glutinous mud to cross.'

'Did you check that in the tide tables?' the inspector asked.

'I don't have to. When you've sailed as long as I have you'll get to know that sort of thing.'

The inspector turned his suspicious eyes on Alan Bunt. 'How did you persuade the lady to go on board?'

'I just asked her to,' Alan said, 'and she agreed. No threats, and no violence, if that's what you mean, Inspector.'

'Humph,' said the inspector. 'Did you lock her in?'

'Certainly not. Even if I'd wanted to, I didn't have a key. But as I've pointed out, she was perfectly willing to disappear for a few hours.'

'It would be hard enough to get out,' I said, 'if you'd tied the covers down.'

'It would, but I didn't. I left them loose on one side, just as I found them.'

'Left that way by Henshel,' I said.

The inspector looked at me. 'Left for . . . But what time was this?'

'Getting on for dark.'

'Then –'

'I just asked Mr Thorne about that,' I said. 'He came very late that day, in the evening. He'd been running gas and foam to a fire that afternoon, so he worked overtime. It was dark when he got here.'

Alan was staring at us. 'What happened?' he asked. His voice shook, and I could see that he had guessed at least a part of the truth.

'Henshel had an arrangement with his own firm, for controlling the fungus infection.' Inspector Plummer spoke gently, with compassion. 'His driver came and shovelled dry ice down through a special hatch into a big locker affair at the back of the heads, and sealed down the covers.'

'Is . . . is that when she died?'

'Yes, of course. Carbon dioxide poisoning. Dead in – how long, Lady P?'

'Quite quickly,' I said. 'She wouldn't know what hit her. She might just think she'd been taken ill.'

'But,' said Alan, 'but wouldn't she have heard him? Why didn't she cry out? But, no,' he added, 'she wouldn't have known what was coming. But surely the driver would have heard someone on board?'

'You knew that she was deaf?' I asked.

'Yes, I did, though I'd forgotten. Her hearing-aid was hidden in the frame of her spectacles.'

'Well, that's the tragedy of it. So's he. Two deaf people, one killing the other, because neither knew the other was there. People with hearing-aids usually keep them switched off when they're alone, to save the batteries.'

I used the short silence to transfer from my pocket to the table a hearing-aid box linked by a thin wire to a pair of broken spectacles.

'Those look like hers,' Alan said.

'Where did you find those?' the inspector asked sharply.

'In your bilge,' I said. 'If you'd done the job properly and taken the ballast out for cleaning and painting you'd have found it yourself. And probably dropped it in the harbour. It was jammed down among the blocks. I'd never have seen it if I hadn't had to duck down after John's knife. You'll notice that it's switched off. When she keeled over, I suppose the box part would have slid out of her cardigan pocket, and the weight on the wire pulled the glasses off her face and the lot went down the back of the bunk into the bilge.'

Inspector Plummer put out his hand and turned the little switch. He tapped the box, but no sound came through the earphone. A year in salt air is too much for most batteries. He sat looking at the mute exhibit. I think he would have liked to relieve his feelings by reproving me for tampering with evidence, but he knows that I always keep my threats.

'It all makes sense,' he said plaintively, 'except the dates. She seemed so fresh. Was she removed to a cold store after all?'

'Nobody knew she was there,' I said. 'No, she was in a cold store to start off with. A comparatively well insulated boat, during an exceptionally cold winter, and, to judge from where I found the spectacles, quite close to the locker – perhaps even in the heads, tidying her hair – into which large quantities of dry ice were deposited at regular intervals.'

'That's cold stuff,' he said gropingly.

'It's very cold stuff indeed,' I said. 'It's not only a gas frozen solid, but in boiling away it has its latent heats of melting and evaporation to recover out of its surroundings. You can take it from me as an engineer that the carbon dioxide coming out of that locker would be cold enough to deep freeze the poor woman. In the weather we

162

had then, by the time she was thawing out the next load would be due. In those conditions, I think she'd keep fresh indefinitely, although you'd have to ask your medical experts about it.'

'I'll have to. But you're an engineer, you should know.' The inspector stared straight ahead at nothing. 'That explains everything up to the spring of this year, with at least some evidence.' He looked more worried than I would have expected. The unravelling of a long-standing mysterious death should have called for a re-action more towards singing and dancing than a furrowed brow.

'Evidence,' I said, 'but not evidence of a crime.'

'True so far. But moving a body, that's a crime. Several, in fact,' he added.

If the posthumous movements of Mrs Gallagher were to be discussed, it was high time that Alan Bunt left the conclave, but if I had tried openly to get rid of him the inspector's suspicions would have reawoken. Instead, I caught the inspector's eye and gave him a warning shake of the head, flicking my eyes towards Alan Bunt, as if to hint that the next part of our discussion might be rather delicate to be held in the presence of a witness whose involvement had now been fully explored . . .

He grabbed the hint like a starving vulture. 'If you've nothing else to add, Mr Bunt . . . ? Then I think we can spare you for now. If the case is reopened, you're on your boat?'

Alan said that he was. He omitted to mention that his boat would have a new mast in a day or two.

'In the meantime, please write me out a statement – as full as you can remember.'

'I will,' said Alan. 'Oh, I will.' He left the room quickly, without meeting my eye. I decided that if I needed him he would not get further than Fowey before the end of the week.

The inspector was looking tired. 'We know who moved the body, don't we?' he said sadly.

I calculated my next moves, but I still failed to see the trap that I was walking into. 'He's a powerful man,' I said warningly.

Inspector Plummer raised his big nose, and squared his shoulders. 'That won't protect him if he's transgressed the law. But it may make it more difficult to prove,' he added.

'You've got the spectacles,' I said. 'Her optician can confirm that they were her lenses.'

'I'm aware of that. But the most that they do is to indicate that she was on the boat at some unspecified time. We need a witness. One witness is often worth a ton of evidence. What's more, a good witness gives grounds for search, and that usually produces the evidence we need. Your friend Geoff Allen, now. You said that he had a story?'

'I . . . I think you'd better hear it for yourself,' I said. I was beginning to realize that my plan of campaign was not going to work out. And now it was too late to invent some trivial story, in Geoff's name, to put the inspector off that particular scent.

'I'll go and see him now,' he said quickly. 'Are you coming with me?'

'I'm late for an appointment,' I said. I left in a hurry, and was very careful to take all of Jackie's notes with me. My hands were shaking, my stomach seemed to be revolving slowly about three different axes, and the muscles of my neck had turned into iron bars.

I made first for the phone-box across the street. *Dawn Breeze* had gone now, and all was quiet. I made a call to Mac, and then I phoned Beau and told him that tonight might be a good night to stay away from home, if anyone would have him.

And then I walked in the dying wind to the office, and locked myself in with Jackie while we carefully expurgated the records covering the dangerous part of the previous spring.

Eleven

B ack at home, a rather tense meeting was held in the Big Room. The tension was provided by myself. Mac was his usual calm, sensible self, and the two lean, dark men in cheap, dark suits showed no emotion as I expounded the day's happenings.

'It's my own damned fault,' I finished bitterly. 'I started off happily assuming that as I stirred things up so the truth would emerge and proof of it would follow – if I was right. It works that way in research, and it's usually so in criminal investigation. But this time I was right in my theory, the truth emerged but I didn't like it when I got it, and the proof that followed proved the wrong blasted part of the facts. We've got perfectly satisfactory evidence as to how the lady came to die, which matters not one scrap in the present situation because she died accidentally and I don't see that anyone could even be charged with negligence.'

Mac nodded. 'But you didna' see that at the time,' he said.

'No, I did not. Evidence was coming forward satisfactorily, and I didn't stop to think that it wasn't supporting what I wanted supported. I went and put my big foot in it. Now, the only real crime that we could have proved is the moving of the body. And the body was moved twice.'

'By Henshel, an' by young Mr Bunt,' said Mac.

'An' ye canna' shop the one without the other,' said one of the men brightly.

166

'That's it exactly,' I said, and they nodded in unison. It seemed to be a situation that they had encountered before.

'But it's worse than that,' I said. 'I was so sure that I could put Henshel away without bail, where he couldn't get back at any of us, that I've put Alan Bunt in danger of another beating, and I've not only put Geoff Allen in the same position but I've put him up to giving false statements which I thought would be only confirmatory. If the whole thing rests on his testimony it'll be under a lot of pressure and it won't stand up for a minute. Then he'll have both Henshel and the law after his blood.'

'We canna' make it work?' Mac asked.

'Not unless we can put Henshel behind bars for a bit. When that sort of thing happens to a man of that type, he's finished. The bubble bursts. People stop trusting him. His associates jump off the bandwagon. He's watched. Other nasty facts come to light. People come forward with them, just to show that they aren't tarred with the same brush.' I heaved a small sigh. 'And I had so much hoped to send you two gentlemen to return a little of the treatment that he had given to Mac and me. And his fruit of course.'

They nodded again, looking solemnly at a small, hard green pear that lay in the centre of the table.

'We could send the boys anyway,' Mac said, 'but we'd never sleep easy for waiting for him to send his ain lads again. You're right enough, Lady P. If we canna' send him inside . . . I suppose we couldna' prove either the corrupt practices or the attacks on ourselves?'

'Not that I can see,' I said, 'and I've thought it over and over.'

'If you've done that, then it's no' possible,' said Mac. 'I've never known you miss a trick, even a dirty one. But I hate to see him gettin' away from us.'

'He doesn't have to,' I said. 'We can still sink him. But it demands a human sacrifice. Me,' I added unhappily.

They looked at me blankly.

'Look at it this way,' I said. 'We know that he sent his boys to beat us up. Well, let's prove that he did it again by fabricating such strong evidence that it's infallible. We gather together everybody that we can think of who hates his guts. You two boys give me a going-over which will be conspicuous without being too painful, and I'm rescued by a dozen witnesses who hear my assailants saying that Henshel sent them. Maybe we could get something traceable back to Henshel to be dropped here – money, perhaps.'

'Clever,' said one of the men, 'but ye'd need more than that. The most of that's still just hearsay.'

'True,' I said. 'Well, we can strengthen it up. Let me think.'

Mac broke in on my thinking. 'But Lady P,' he wailed, 'ye canna'.'

'I can, Mac. I'm not particularly keen to, but I certainly can.'

'Let me do it,' he said desperately.

'You can't,' I said gently. 'First because I wouldn't let you. And secondly because it wouldn't be believed. You see, there's no reason for Henshel to send his goons after you again. You've been a good little Mac and kept your nose out of his affairs. At least, I hope you have?'

'I have. And yoursel'?'

'If I get another hiding, I can make out a pretty good motive against Henshel, because I was asking his driver questions this morning about how Mrs Gallagher died. They implicated Henshel in the moving of the body, and Inspector Plummer was there at the time. So even if they denied that Mr Thorne told him, well, it's what they could be expected to say anyway.'

'And if Mr Thorne really did tell him?' Mac asked quietly. One of the two men grunted.

I probably sat and gaped at him, for the thought hit me like a blow. Somehow it had never occurred to me that Mr Thorne, who had carried tales to his master once, was bound to do so again. And it was a welcome thought. I have no particular fear of physical pain, and without the added fear of the unknown I could easily have nerved myself to tolerate a mild beating of my own specification. But I would much rather not.

'I'm glad someone thought of that,' I said shakily. 'It just hadn't occurred to me. And I could so easily have had them walk in on me here just after I'd taken a beating from you two.' They grinned. 'It wouldn't have been funny,' I added.

'I nearly didna' say anything,' Mac said. 'I could not believe you'd not thought of that yourself. Do you think they're mebbe on their way?'

'I think they probably are,' I said. 'Now that you point out the probability . . . If Thorne told Henshel immediately after we first questioned him, and Henshel phoned London – and what I'd give for a tape of that call! – then if they left at once by car they could easily be here by now, waiting for you to go away. Or they could arrive at any time from now on.'

The two Glasgow lads brightened up, scenting a good scrap, but it was not to be. My wits were making up for their previous dullness. I had one of my rare periods of blazing enlightenment, riding on the crest of a brainwave. In less than ten seconds of this cerebral surf-ride I saw my whole plan in clear detail, with every variant neatly charted and with critical path programmes for the trickier bits.

'We'd better get your car away,' I said, 'and show them an empty house. But first you'd better see the layout, and meet the dogs. Especially meet the dogs.'

Mac drove off in his little rattletrap. I locked the house up tight, leaving only the garage doors open, and took the two Glaswegians away in my Cortina.

'They wouldn't leave their car in the road,' I said as I swung out of the drive. 'There's an old track crosses the road just ahead. It's the logical place to park a car where it won't be noticed. If you'll just take a look, one to each side, without turning the heads more than necessary . . . Here we are!'

We passed the lane. The man on my left gave an affirmative grunt.

'Ah,' I said. 'Can you start a locked car?'

'Aye. Nae bother.' He produced a screwdriver and a length of wire from an inside pocket.

'Well,' I said, 'that saves me giving you a lesson in the pub car park.'

We met Mac by arrangement in the Star and Candle, and we settled down in separate bars to wait for dusk. It would be as well if Mac and I were not seen with the Glasgow boys any more than strictly necessary.

While Mac ate salted peanuts and sipped his beer, I chewed over every detail of my plan, polishing its refinements to a high gloss. I always think best at a bar. In the Seminar Room of the Department of Zoology at the university there is a display entitled 'Natural Habitats', and among the elephants in long grass and wallabies in blue gums my photograph has been included. I am shown on a stool at the Staff Club bar, glass in hand and deep in thought, and I take it as a high compliment.

When the light was down to a slowly fading glow that barely touched the earth but silhouetted trees that still moved in the dying wind, we met at my car. Mac got in with us.

'They shouldn't be waiting in the garage,' I said, 'because I'd see them in the headlights and I could back straight out again. But if they are, it'll be a rough house. What they want, however, is to catch me outside the car. If they've broken into the house somewhere that the dogs can't get at them, the dogs will warn me.'

'Doped or poisoned meat?' said Mac.

'I don't think so. When those dogs get excited they don't eat. So what my visitors would probably do is to wait outside, either to follow me into the garage or to lure me outside. Now, in the unlikely event that—'

And I laid it all on the line for them, step by step, and went over it again and again until I was sure that they knew their parts in every foreseeable situation.

Mac drove his own car to the old track, and there left it with the key in the ignition, on the opposite side of the road from the car that we had seen. We others detoured slightly on the way, in order that Henshel's imposing house in the suburbs of Downfield might be pointed out. I was pleased to note that the windows were blazing with lights – my fear had been that Henshel might be establishing his alibi away from home, forcing me to adopt one of my more elaborate plans.

Mac was waiting at the end of the track, deep in the shadows. As I stopped, he slipped into the seat beside me, vacated by one of the men who slipped silently into the trees and returned. 'Ready tae go,' he said.

I handed Mac the keys of the house, and drove forward. Mac crouched low beside me and, in the back, the two men were down on their knees.

My stomach was fluttering with nerves. And, I must admit, with exhilaration. Revenge, like any other immoral act, can be very sweet.

I turned in at the gate. In a moment I would know for sure that they had come, unless the car in the track was nothing but one of the coincidences that I had dismissed so lightly.

And then I knew that we were right. They had come. In front of the house, not far from the garage doors, a dustbin lid lay on the gravel, rolling in circles as the wind toyed with it. I rounded it carefully. My headlights flooded the empty garage as I entered it.

The gun came with me as I left the car, and was in my waistband by the time I reached the garage doors. I walked loudly to drown the stealthy noises behind me, and I came out again into the faint light, praying that the others would remember their parts. The dustbin lid scraped round in another oscillation, grinding out a noise calculated to drive any householder mad. As naturally as I could, I stooped for it. By now, Mac should have the house-door from the garage unlocked. Dear God, please don't let those stupid dogs mistake him for an invader, I thought.

Only because I was expecting them, I heard their foot-steps approaching over the drumming of my heartbeats. I swung round. This was the dangerous moment.

They came at me together, the same two men, big and dark against the white wall. I yelled, and kept on yelling. At this point, I wanted no misunderstandings.

As soon as I gave tongue, and just as the men grabbed me by an arm apiece, light flooded from the lamp over the front door and came pouring from the open garage.

Out of the garage, too, came a pair of fiends, crouched and deadly, teeth bared ready for a taste of blood. They sprinted in a silence broken only by the scuff of gravel and an occasional gargle that was more terrifying than a full blooded baying could ever have been.

They froze on either side of me, my two assailants, for a moment that might easily have cost them a limb apiece.

'Run,' I shouted, 'run. I don't want your blood on my hands.' As their hands fell from me, I pulled out the pistol. If either man looked like carelessly getting killed, I would have to scare the dogs off and play it cowboy style. If either man lifted a gun against the dogs, I'd blow a hole in his head. And if he lifted his foot, he'd lose it.

They broke and ran. 'Faster,' I shouted after them. 'I don't want blood in the dogs' fur either.'

One man made for the trees. He probably had the big sycamore in mind, but Cressida was near and my apple tree was nearer. He made it into the upper branches an inch ahead of Cressida's fangs. The other ran for the road, realized that he had misjudged Sol's speed and swerved for the apple tree, found it occupied and Cressida waiting, and hurled himself towards the fence beside the field. His second swerve as he ran into a clothes-line threw Sol off his distance, but the second slashing run in brought a pandemonium of noise – snarls, a bellow and the sound of tearing cloth. I raised the gun to fire a shot and scare the dogs away, but Sol's speed had carried him past and in the instant that it took him to turn the man raised himself, apparently by levitation, up to the top of a high gate which, for some long forgotten reason, stands in the middle of the fence.

I walked over to the gate, carrying the gun in a prominent position. The gate is topped by several twisted strands of rusty barbed wire, and the man had found some sort of sanctuary lying prone along the barbs. It was not a haven that I would have chosen myself, but then, I have never been savaged by a Borzoi. The man, at least, seemed to prefer it to the ground, and looking at Sol's snarl at close quarters I could see that he had a point of view.

The next phase of the operation demanded the consumption of a certain amount of time, for Mac had to telephone Inspector Plummer – of necessity from the phone box down the road – while one of his friends locked up the house and then broke into it again and the other stood guard in the background. The inspector was to be warned to approach with stealth. In the meantime, I would play on their already quivering nerves.

A clothes-line prop was nearby. I fetched it, and poked the fence-hanger in the ribs. Even in the dim light, I could see that this must be the stockier of my previous assailants. 'Throw down your gun,' I said, 'or I'll poke you off and let them eat you.'

I saw his eyes rolling in a daintily innocent moon-face. 'No gun. If I 'ad, I'd 'a' used it by now,' he said hoarsely, and I recognized his slightly fluting voice.

'Well, I've got one,' I said, 'so if you've got one hidden keep it hidden. One false move and the dogs have you for supper. And breakfast,' I added thoughtfully, for he seemed to be even heavier than I had judged.

'Call them beasts off, missis,' he said plaintively. 'I won't give no trouble.'

'Well, bully for you,' I said. 'But you're living in a dreamworld.' As I spoke, Sol made a scrambling leap up the gate, missing the man's arm by a margin that seemed precariously small. His startled withdrawal nearly toppled the man off his perch, and I heard something tear on the barbed wire. 'I may bring him out a box to take off from,' I said reflectively.

'You wouldn't do that?'

'Don't kid yourself. What would you do, if you were me?'

I left him to think that one out and crossed to the apple tree, taking my prop with me. In that light Cressida looked like some demon from the pit, and her teeth were like those in the jaws of a bear-trap. The thin face that peered down through the branches was very white.

'You call the dogs off, or you'll be sorry when we get down.'

I laughed. 'If you get down, you'll be sorrier.' I gave him, too, a good poke with the end of my prop, and

Cressida, with a snarl like ripping cloth, leaped seven feet straight up. 'If you break one twig of my tree,' I said, 'I'll feed you to her over a period of weeks.'

I heard the man sigh. 'All right,' he said, 'you've had your fun. It's a fair cop. Now call the fuzz.' His voice was still scratchy, but it was a lot less deep than it had been, the last time that I heard it.

'I'll call them in my own good time,' I said. 'In a week or two.'

It was the fence-hanger behind me who spoke first. 'A week or two?' he squawked. 'You can't keep us up here that long.'

'Of course she can't,' the man in the tree said impatiently. 'Don't let her get up your—' I never found out exactly what of his the other man was not to let me get up, for the sentence was broken off abruptly as Cressida made a cunning, silent leap at an incautiously gestured hand, and was only robbed of her pound of flesh by a violent reaction that sent an ominous creak through the whole tree.

'I don't see why I can't,' I said. 'Nobody ever comes up here. The occasional car goes past, of course, but if you start shouting the dogs will drown you out anyway . . .'

'Your nephew comes here, doesn't he? He lives here.'

'He does. But I can't see him interceding for you. You see, he found me after your last visit here. The only difference is that he's so particular about the dogs' diet that he'll probably insist on putting you through the mincer before feeding you to them. And,' I added, 'don't count on making a run for it in the dark. These beasts depend more on their ears and noses than their eyes when they're running down a quarry. In your case, noses. They'll have the guts out of you, if you'll pardon the expression, before you've gone ten yards.'

At that point I was called one or two names. Rude

though they were, they were names I had been called before and doubtless would be again and in the ordinary way I would have ignored them as improbable and uninspired, but in the interests of general agitation I decided that it was incumbent on me to do a little more prodding with the prop. So I prodded, with interesting and nearly lethal results, but I prodded absently while cross-checking my arrangements. By now Inspector Plummer must be on his way or Mac would have contacted me again. So Mac would be at an upper window of the house, watching one of his fellow Scots who, near my victims' car, was waiting to signal the approach of the inspector and his blue flasher. The other Scot was nearer at hand, to see where Inspector Plummer parked his car.

The long pruner was accessible, in the shed this side of the garage, so I fetched it as a substitute for the clothes prop and went to have a look at the man on the gate. Sol seemed to be gaining height with practice, or else the barbed wire was taking its toll, for trickles of blood looked black in the poor light. 'You can't keep us up 'ere forever,' he said faintly. 'Them dogs . . .'

'I've seen them dogs wait for days under a cat,' I said. 'They take it in turns. They're very intelligent, in a limited way.'

I went back to the tree. Its inhabitant seemed to be getting off rather lightly, so I started pruning around him. 'It's a pity you didn't take to the gate,' I said. 'It would have burned beautifully.'

He spat at me, but without range or precision.

'My best advice to you,' I said, 'would be not to offer any provocation. You burned me, remember? Some petrol and some old timber, and you could take your choice between being eaten raw or flambé.' I continued pruning. As the smaller branches were snipped away from around him he seemed to lose the last shreds of his sense of security, and he cursed me and the world in a voice that he would never have recognized as his own. He also rashly grabbed the end of the pruner.

I pulled, quite gently. The main branch bowed slowly with a low groan and then paused. The man froze, not daring even to cringe as Cressida's teeth clanged beside his face. He still held the pruner, so I worked its handle to and fro. He let loose a scream that sent the dogs into a frenzy.

'That was my finger,' he said as the pandemonium died down.

'It still is,' I said. 'Do you want it back?'

He shook the injured member cautiously, spattering bloodspots around. I had the impression that he was weeping, but he still managed to utter a naughty word that could just, by an extreme stretching of the imagination, be construed as applicable to myself. So I poked him, again quite gently, between the legs with the end of the pruner. I also waggled the handle noisily, although refraining from giving it that drastic tug.

This time, he surpassed all previous efforts. His wild ululation made the hair creep on my neck; and Mac, who materialized beside me at that moment, looked more shaken than I had seen him but also looked pleased. He had suffered, too.

Mac pulled my sleeve. 'Arriving,' he whispered, and gave me back my keys.

It was time that Councillor Henshel's name was dragged into the conversation. 'Next time, I'll do it,' I said. 'You will have a tale to tell, won't you?'

He took the bait beautifully. 'You just wait until Mr Henshel hears about this,' he said weakly.

I laughed, and Mac joined in. 'Henshel won't mind,' I said. I spoke quickly and loudly, for there was a car's engine not far away. This had to be said before the inspector arrived, and Mac and I would have to deny it on oath if need be – the rules of evidence being what I believe them to be. 'Mr Henshel and I are the best of pals.'

'If . . . then why . . . ?'

I laughed again. Now I knew that I was going to bring it off. 'Mr Henshel and I have a business deal going about something else. He knew I was putting the screw on hard, just because he sent you after me once before, but he wants what I'm selling. But he knew that I had it in for you two as well.' I was speaking softly now, for two dark shadows were approaching silently over the grass. 'So . . . he sold you to me as part of the deal.'

There was a stunned silence, just long enough to let the inspector and his constable get well within earshot. And then they cut loose, both of them.

If I had written the script myself, it could not have been more perfect. In two minutes of impassioned verbosity they admitted that Henshel had paid them to assault myself and Mac, they accused Henshel of sending them into a trap, and they announced the many and remarkable things they would do to the councillor when they got their hands on him. They added that they would thereafter shop him if they shopped themselves at the same time.

The two officers stopped and listened in silence. Over their shoulders I saw a blue flash through the trees, and it was not the lamp on the roof of the car. I hoped very much that they had left the car unguarded – otherwise some young constable was likely to be lying on his face, nursing a case of incipient concussion.

It was time to play the rest of the hand. 'Will you take over now, Inspector?' I called.

He came out of the shadows. 'I certainly will,' he said grimly, and took his time examining the two men. The dogs sensibly ignored him and lay quiet, watching their targets with baleful and unwinking eyes. 'As I thought,' he said. 'Snotty Yarmouth and Face Flanders. Nice to have an inspired guess confirmed. Well, it's my pleasant duty to tell you that anything you say will be taken down and may be used in evidence. And you are not obliged to say anything. Not, if you don't want to get down,' he added.

My jaw dropped, but the constable winked at me. 'I didn't hear that bit,' he muttered.

I held my breath, for a statement made after a formal caution is worth ten made before. But I might as well have breathed. My plump friend on the gate – 'Snotty' as I must now learn to call him – resumed his sad song, begging the inspector to rescue him from the desperate situation into which he had been plunged. He went into a lot of unnecessary detail about it, but we let him ramble. The other, 'Face', was more succinct. That bastard Henshel, he said, had sent him straight into a trap when he commissioned him to rough up her ladyship again, and if he ever saw the louse again he'd flatten him.

It was all very satisfactory.

'All right,' said the inspector at last, and there was a special satisfaction in his voice which I only understood later. 'You can come down now.'

'Not as long as them dogs are loose,' said a plaintive voice.

'Shall I get rid of them?' I asked.

'Please do,' said the inspector.

He intended, I think, that I should leash the dogs and hold them in reserve, but he should have said so. For my plan, it was desirable that at least one of the men should be free, for a while.

I pointed the gun down into the grass, and pulled the trigger.

Two dark shapes fled yelping into the shadows. They were out of sight in an instant, but their voices could be heard diminishing across the fields.

A bigger shape dropped stiffly out of the apple tree. Another rolled, with the sound of tearing cloth and a gasp of pain, down from the gate. They ran, stumbling, on converging courses but in the general direction of the road.

The inspector surprised me by remaining motionless at my side, but the constable dashed of after the fugitives. We heard noises, from beyond our range of vision.

'That was very naughty of you,' the inspector said, without the least trace of anger.

Engine noises could be heard now from a distance. As the constable came panting back, nursing what looked, given time, would develop into a fine specimen of the cauliflower ear, I embarked on a long explanation and apology for my accidental discharge of the gun. Not that I gave a damn for the inspector's forgiveness, but I hoped that my voice would conceal the sound of not one but two cars driving away – the two Scots in the car belonging to, or at least in the possession of, Messrs Flanders and Yarmouth, and those two gentlemen, I hoped, having seen their car drive off under their noses, departing in Mac's car which had been left for the purpose. This was an unnecessary elaboration of my plot, but it would help to provide a little more corroborative evidence.

'I tried, Sir,' said the constable.

'No man can do more,' said the inspector.

The constable asked whether he should get on the radio.

'Radio?' It seemed to me that the inspector was behaving very oddly.

'Sir, you heard them threaten to go after Mr Henshel . . .'

'So I did. Yes indeed. All right, go and use the radio.'

The constable, who seemed to suffer from an excess of zeal, dashed off. We followed more slowly. In the drive, the constable was sitting in a very dark car. He seemed to be upset about something. 'Sir,' he said, 'the battery's flat.'

'I wonder how that happened,' said the inspector.

Speaking as an engineer, I could have told him that it had happened because a spanner had been laid across the terminals, but I held my peace.

The constable jumped up out of the car. 'May I use your phone?' he asked on the way past.

'Help yourself,' I called after his retreating back.

We walked after him again. The inspector still seemed to be emanating a quiet amusement, but it was nothing that I could challenge.

Mac, who had faded discreetly into the background, was waiting beside the broken window. 'Your laddie went in this way,' he said.

'He didn't—?'

'Na,' Mac said reluctantly. 'It was broken afore. I doubt those two men . . .'

'Nae doubt,' said the inspector, and Mac turned very quiet.

I used my key, and we met the constable inside the front door. 'The phone's been pulled out and wrecked,' he said.

The inspector sighed, looking at his own reflection in the mirror over the hall table. 'Perhaps Lady P would give us a lift down to the local shop,' he said.

'Delighted,' I said.

I got the Cortina out again, and drove them down to the police station. The inspector was very calm, but his subordinate seemed to be in an agony of impatience. I dropped them at the door, and went back for Mac. He was waiting at the gate.

'It all went off very well,' he said, dropping his small frame down lightly beside me. 'Do ye think—?'

'We'll soon know,' I said. I took the ring road for a mile or two, and then looped through an expensive estate of large new houses. Before we reached Henshel's Spanish-style horror an ambulance passed us, heading into town. Two policemen were outside his house, but they were paying no attention to the car abandoned two houses further on.

'All according to plan,' I said. 'This calls for a celebration.'

For a calculated interval of forty minutes, we drank sparingly in the first hotel in a Londonward direction from Henshel's house. Then Mac called the police and reported his car stolen from the car park outside.

Twelve

L ater in the same week, the inspector walked in on me in the kitchen, where I was preparing some slurp for Toots who was temporarily in my care again, and at the same time thinking over an idea for a new cheap air-conditioner.

'You'd better take a seat in here,' I said. 'I'm not feeding this messy brute over a carpet.'

He sat down at the kitchen table. 'I've never seen you look so domesticated,' he said.

'This isn't the real me,' I said shortly. I had an uncomfortable hunch that I knew what the trend of the inspector's conversation would be. I started spooning food into my grandson, in silence.

'They were caught just this side of London,' the inspector said suddenly. 'In Mr MacKillop's old car.'

'It was the same people who stole Mac's old crock, then?'

'You don't have to simulate surprise if it's an effort,' he said. 'But, yes, that's a good enough supposition to go along with, although I have my doubts as to whether it happened just as we're meant to believe. My personal doubts, that is. We found a stolen car abandoned, near Mr Henshel's house, as if your two friends had got that far, broken down, abandoned it and stolen another.'

'And you don't accept that?' While my attention was distracted, one of Toots' chubby fists caught the spoon and splattered me with guck.

'There's no need to call him things like that,' the inspector said reprovingly. 'I think you'd better let me feed him – you don't seem to have the touch at all.' He pulled the high chair round, and went on, 'No, I don't accept it. The whole affair has the smell of a frame-up to me.'

'I don't follow you,' I said. 'I read in the papers that Councillor Henshel had been attacked and beaten up, and in view of what we heard those men say I wasn't very surprised, but that's all I know.'

'Maybe,' he said. 'Come on, little fellow. Take one for Mummy – but looking at it through your devious eyes, I think you had the whole thing planned. Henshel certainly got a beating, and something rather nasty was done to him with a hard, green pear. And I remembered you saying that he'd get his fruit back – and one for Daddy – and there I was presented with two demoralized men carefully programmed to spill enough information to put Henshel away.'

'What about the cars, then?'

'You couldn't be sure that they really would go after Henshel, so you sent two other boys in the car your attackers – or should I say victims? – had come in. But you made it easy for those two poor suckers to get away in the slowest and most conspicuous car available to you. Would it surprise you to know that they deny going near Henshel?'

'What else would you expect them to say?' I asked.

'Oh, nothing, nothing – take one for your clever Granny, now – or that Henshel swears that the men who attacked him were complete strangers, with strong Scottish accents?'

'Again, of course he'd deny knowing them,' I said.

'Come along, old boy,' he said, 'take one for the nice policeman.' Toots disappointed me by accepting it. 'But,

you see, I don't particularly want to prove it. I like it the way it stands at present.'

'I . . . I don't think I quite understand,' I said.

He shot the last mouthful neatly into my gra 'You'd better take him away and hose him down or thing,' he said. 'No, not now. I'd be happier in my if you didn't pick him up until I've had my say daughter would never forgive me if I made you dro and I'm rather dependent on her for chandlery moment.

'A lot happened after our discussion at St Marg Your Mr Thorne told Henshel that we were asking tions – you must have guessed that. So, as well as se his boys to you, he started pulling strings arour county. He had a lot of influential friends, although t all renouncing him now. And my boss sent for m told me that I was a damned fool, that as far as h concerned I could abandon all hope of making inspector, and that if I ever even mentioned Mr Hen sacred name again he would consider it an act of phemy and bust me down to something just below a warden. Those weren't his exact words, but they're enough to the gist of it. What's more, he said it presence of certain other parties, not all of whom friends of Henshel even before his fall from grace.

'I begin to see,' I said. I fetched a cloth, and wiping Toots over.

'I thought you might. My hands were pretty well but I had no particular fondness for Henshel and a feeling that if justice was being done it was "done" other sense of the word. So when I got Mr MacKi call, and came out and found two men implicating He with every breath, it was like a gift from heaven.'

'And, of course,' I said, 'that's why you weren't i particular hurry to send a bodyguard out to his hous

'Now that,' he said reprovingly, 'is just the kind of thing you mustn't say, just as I have no intention of showing any disbelief in the nice neat case which is now reflecting glory on me and discredit on my boss. And just to be sure that you say nothing that's not in the script – and that means nothing about the matter of the evidence now recovered from the bottom of the harbour as well – I'm keeping a photocopy of this.'

'Yes,' I said. 'I wondered if you had it. I noticed you pause by the hall table.'

'You'd better pay it,' he said. 'But if you say anything to throw doubt on the case against Henshel, I'll be free to use it. You understand?'

I said that I understood, and he gave me back an account from my travel agent for two BEA tickets from Prestwick via Heathrow.

I still regret one mistake that I made during the affair. One part of my plan rebounded on me. I had underestimated the value of my own work. It had occurred to Henshel, as it never did to me, that if the many secondhand Bentleys and other large and luxurious cars on the market could be induced to do around thirty-five miles on one of today's expensive gallons, their value could be enhanced enormously. There will be a tidy sum waiting for him, when Her Majesty is at last pleased to release him.